MW01204747

TOMORROW'S WISHES

•

DIANA FOX

AVALON BOOKS
THOMAS BOUREGY AND COMPANY, INC.
401 LAFAYETTE STREET
NEW YORK, NEW YORK 10003

PRINTED IN THE UNITED STATES OF AMERICA
ON ACID-FREE PAPER
BY HADDON CRAFTSMEN, SCRANTON, PENNSYLVANIA

TOMORROW'S
WISHES

Chapter One

"When a man loves a woman...." Michael Bolton's voice vibrated through the apartment.

With her hands on her hips, Marion Winter blew a tired breath of air toward her bangs. Wisps of dark-colored hair stirred, floating upward, then dropped back into place. In all her twenty-six years, she'd never cleaned a more masculine bedroom.

Barbells and a weight-lifting machine filled one corner of the average-size room. The short shag carpet was rust colored, the walls a complementary cream. Floor-to-ceiling wooden shelves filled another corner. The shelves held gleaming trophies, balls representative of every sport, including a baseball signed by Babe Ruth and a basketball signed by Michael Jordan. Golf clubs, a tennis racket, and other sports paraphernalia stood tidily in a third corner. And a dozen pair of sport shoes in various stages of wear were lined neatly on the closet floor.

A king-size bed with a mammoth pecan headboard filled the remainder of the room. Marion had changed the spotted leopard sheets for those in the pattern of a pride of lions. A bedspread of zebra stripes now hid the pride.

When Marion had first entered the room, she'd been appalled that anyone could live in such a mess. But then, the bedroom shouldn't have surprised her. The rest of the apartment had been just as messy.

In the beginning when she had started her cleaning business, Maid Marion, she had expected bachelors to make up the bulk of her clientele. But in eight months' time, John Dalton was her first bachelor.

Judging from his belongings, Marion decided John Dalton was a walking contradiction. Her father had met him when he came to the house to sign her contract and drop off a set of keys, but described him only as tall and wearing glasses. She had yet to meet her newest client.

Usually, it was easy to form a picture of a home's owner by their possessions. But John Dalton's image kept changing.

Her first impression of him had been that of an artist—thin, wearing a Hawaiian shirt or old T-shirts stamped *Northeastern College*. This image formed when she saw the drafting board, surrounded by brushes, pens, and paper strewn everywhere, occupying a corner of the living room. The table-like structure sat in front of the sliding glass door that led to a balcony, bare save for one outdoor chair. Past experience told her to leave that area of the room, obviously a work space, alone until she received specific instructions on how to clean it, so she had bypassed that part of the room.

When she stepped into his bedroom, her second image of John Dalton had been that of Hulk Hogan. Not only had it resembled a men's locker room, but it had smelled like one too.

But the real surprise had come when she had opened his closet and found more than a dozen business suits, hanging neatly. The closet was the only thing in the whole apartment that had some order to it.

John Dalton had to be a cross between Hulk Hogan, George Lucas, and William F. Buckley, Jr., she decided. But whatever image he fit, he was a slob.

The bathroom had been a nightmare. She shuddered at the thought of what she'd find in the kitchen, the last room to be cleaned.

Turning away from the bedroom, she bent and retrieved her carry-all basket of supplies. Head bent, she inspected the basket, holding it in front of her as she walked down the hallway, reminding herself that she needed to refill her glass cleaner.

Suddenly, her movement stopped, the basket crushing into her midsection.

Surprised, Marion looked up. Shock ran through her, her skin turned cold with fear, and the air left her lungs. The wall she had run into was no wall. It was a man. He stood about six-three to her five-six. A strand of dark hair lay curled on his forehead. Equally dark brows hooded eyes the color of milk chocolate, and his gaze bore into her. His impressively wide shoulders made the narrow three-foot hall width seem even narrower.

"Who in blue blazes are you?" he asked.

His voice rumbled loudly against the walls of the hall.

"Maid Marion," she said.

"Yeah, right. And I'm Robin Hood."

"No, I really am Maid Marion," she repeated. "Marion Winter, actually." She saw nothing but puzzlement in his eyes. "Maid Marion is the name of my business. I presume you're John Dalton." He nodded. "You hired me to clean your house."

"I did no such thing. How did you get in here?"

"You left your keys with my father."

"I've never met your father."

"Yes, you did, Mr. Dalton. Two nights ago."

"And I'm telling you, I didn't."

Marion bit her lip. Nothing made sense. Remembering the contract, she moved forward, intending to go to the small table near the entrance, but he blocked her way.

"Where are you going?"

"To get the contract you signed."

For a long moment he studied her, then silently he turned sideways. Marion swung the basket in front of her in an attempt to bring the bulky item in line with her body, and in the process, her knuckles rubbed against the front of his powder-blue chambray shirt. She felt his stomach muscles contract and heard his short inhalation of air.

She darted a quick look at him, puzzled at the heat she had first felt in her knuckles that now radiated throughout the rest of her body. Startled by the intensity of his expression, she pressed forward, determined to get past him without further incident.

Reaching the small oak table near the door, she set the basket on the floor and reached for the canvas bag that acted as her traveling office wherever she went. In it she carried the records of her clients and other pertinent information she needed from day to day. Quickly, she found what she was looking for and extracted two sheets of stapled paper.

She believed in brevity and organization, and her contracts reflected her philosophy. Turning, she was surprised to see John Dalton standing behind her. She held the papers out to him, and he took them.

She watched as he scanned through the material, turning to the second page. His gaze dropped to the bottom of the page to the signature line. His mouth a straight line, he glanced at her, then spun around.

In half a dozen steps he was at the drafting table. She followed. He reached for a pen and scribbled something at the bottom of the page, dropped the pen, straightened, and turned back to her.

With the papers back in her possession she looked at what he had written. His name was scribbled, almost unreadable, below the first signature.

"They're not the same," she said.

"I told you they weren't."

"But who—"

"I don't know. All I know is that I didn't arrange for your services."

"I believe you, Mr. Dalton."

"John, please. I'm not old enough to be called mister." He smiled.

It was a nice smile, she thought. She especially liked the tiny dimple that appeared at the left side of his mouth.

"As a bachelor, John, you could use my services."

"How do you know I'm a bachelor?"

"You—I mean, your impersonator—told my father you were. Was he lying?"

He seemed to hesitate. Was he hiding a wife and kids? she wondered.

"No. I'm a bachelor. Bona fide."

Whatever that meant. She saw him notice the apartment, seemingly for the first time since he entered the rooms. He appeared stunned.

"I hardly recognize the place," he said.

"I'm not surprised," she told him. "But I didn't touch your work area. I've learned from experience to get permission to straighten a desk, no matter how disgustingly unorganized it is."

John's gaze returned to Marion. "You like organization, don't you?"

"It's my job."

"And you do it very well."

Marion took that as a compliment. "But ...?" Though he hadn't said it, she knew there was a but on the end of his sentence.

"But I won't be needing your services anymore."

"I haven't finished. I was going to do the kitchen next. It was the last room."

"That's okay," he told her. "Let's pretend that you did."

Marion shook her head. "I couldn't do that. I was paid to clean your apartment twice a week."

"Then refund the money."

"I can't do that. The gentleman paid in cash."

"Then think of it as a bonus."

"I can't do that either. I wouldn't feel right."

"Then let me find out who did this and when I do, you can make the refund then."

Marion swallowed. This was becoming more and more difficult. "I still couldn't make the refund. I used the money as a down payment on my van. I needed it for my business. My hatchback was too small and too old. I'm sorry." She wished now that she hadn't been so quick to purchase the automobile, but she'd been so excited to meet her goal of five new clients that month. And the van had been the reward of that goal, an earmark in her career that was now showing steady growth. If she continued garnering new clients at this rate, she'd be able to hire an employee soon. It would probably start as a part-time position, but the way the business was growing, it could turn into a full-time position quickly.

"I see," John said.

Marion chewed on her lip. John had the right to cancel the contract. Even though he didn't sign it, it bore his name and he didn't want the service. If she had to she would make the refund. It would take a little time, but she could do it. She waited for John to tell her she was done. Maybe it was just as well. She didn't like the way her heart skipped a beat every time she looked at him.

"How long will you be cleaning my apartment?"

She widened her eyes in surprise. "Three months." She held her breath. Was it possible that she was going to keep the job?

"All right," he agreed.

Marion smiled, not believing her good luck. "I promise you won't regret your decision."

"I guess I ought to be grateful to my anonymous benefactor," he said. "I'm not the neatest person in the world."

She grinned—she couldn't help herself. "I noticed." She had the job! It was all she could do to keep from jumping up and down, but she held a rein on the emotion. "Are there any special instructions?"

John shook his head. "No, not really. You're doing an excellent job." His smile widened, and his dimple deepened.

When he smiled like that, he looked as if he had stepped out of the clothing section pages of the J. C. Penney catalog, she thought. With his good looks he could have easily been a male model, but the still-messy corner behind him told her he was an artist of some kind.

Her gaze went to that part of the room. "Do you want that area cleaned?" she asked.

He glanced at the corner. "You mean my place of work?"

"You work here?"

His head swiveled back until he was looking at her again. "Is that so unusual?"

"No, not really. Not in this day and age. What do you do?"

"I'm a cartoonist. Among other things."

"Have I ever seen your work before?"

"You have if you read the newspapers. I do political satire."

"Don't you have to be in New York or Washington, D.C. for that type of work? Briar, Georgia seems an unlikely place for a cartoonist."

"I'm a free-lancer. But even from here I can stay abreast of the world's events. Briar may be a small Georgia community, but it's not at the edge of the world."

He was right. Tallahassee, Florida was just thirty-five miles south and Macon and Atlanta were easily reached in three to five hours. He just didn't look like a cartoonist to her—more like a linebacker for the Falcons.

She didn't want to look like she was in a hurry; she had two hours before her next client's appointment, but by the time she was finished with John's kitchen her two hours would be up. "Getting back to my original question."

"Ah, yes, my workstation. I guess it'd be best if you left it alone."

"All right. Will Mondays and Thursdays be okay?"

"As long as you come after three, it is."

She hesitated.

"Is that going to be a problem?" he asked.

"Actually, yes."

"Is there any day you can come after three?"

"On Tuesday, but I can't any other afternoon. I've got other commitments."

Now it was John's turn to hesitate. "I don't imagine you work evenings?"

"No, again I have other commitments."

"Saturdays?"

Marion was about to say no, when she reconsidered. She couldn't be too difficult. He had given in about the contract, after all. If she wanted his business, she had to give a little too. "Sure, Saturday morning is fine."

He stuck out his hand, and she put her

hand in his. The warm touch surprised her. She glanced at their two hands now joined. His hand was a deep shade of golden brown. If he worked during the day indoors, how was it he was so tanned? She noticed the golden hairs on the back of his hand, and that his nails were clean and cut fairly short.

A tingling sensation traveled up her arm. Her gaze flew to his face. It shook her to see him studying her as intently as she'd been studying him.

She pulled her hand away. Now she had to wonder if she had imagined the heat. The tingling sensation happened when he squeezed her fingers. *That's all,* she told herself.

"If you'll excuse me, I've got to get back to work." She moved toward her basket she'd left by the front door.

"And I'll get out of your hair," he said, following her. "I've got some errands to run." He opened the door. "You'll be here Saturday then, right?"

Somewhere down the hall another door opened. A baby wailed. Marion froze.

"Marion?"

It happened every time she heard a baby cry or saw a baby. Her doctor had told her it would take time, but it had been over a year now.

"Marion?"

"Oh...I...I'm sorry. Did you say something?"

"Are you all right?"

"Sure. Sure, what could be wrong?" She shook off the oppression that had threatened to consume her. She wouldn't think about her problem. She had work to do; she'd concentrate on that instead.

John frowned at her. She gave him a bright smile, a smile she didn't wholly feel. He wasn't buying it. "John," she said in her most reassuring tone of voice, "I'm fine."

He looked like he still doubted her. Finally, he said, "I'll see you Saturday."

When the door finally closed, she dropped the basket on the table and leaned against the wall. She couldn't go through life hating babies.

No, that wasn't correct. She didn't hate babies. She just hated the fact she couldn't have one herself.

Chapter Two

Marion arrived home tired and yearning for a long soak in the tub. When she went into the kitchen to fetch a glass of lemonade, she found her father, a widower, on the phone.

A minute later he hung up.

"That was Betty," he said.

Betty was their across-the-street neighbor, a widow about her father's age. Attractive-looking and friendly enough, Marion thought. Actually, her father was friends with all the neighbors, as most of them had lived here for years. Betty's husband died three years ago of a stroke, and

Marion remembered how both her mother and father had helped Betty through her loss.

"She called to tell me about the meeting tonight."

Marion grimaced. "I forgot all about it." Her long soak in the tub just became a short hot shower instead.

During the last two weeks the neighborhood had been in an uproar when they'd learned the vacant lot next to her father's house had been sold and the new owner intended to turn it into a baseball field for the town's children.

The last thing she wanted was a bunch of noisy kids next door, during all hours of the day and into the night. Night games meant bright lights. The quiet streets wouldn't be quiet any longer—the traffic would increase and no doubt there'd be litter left on the grounds. The Millers, two doors down, had said they'd heard a concession stand was going to be built too.

"Did you have any lunch, Dad?"

"I wasn't hungry."

Marion wasn't surprised by his answer. This wasn't the first time he'd gone without his lunch, and yet he looked fit and healthy.

Opening the refrigerator to get her lemonade, she saw the tuna-fish sandwich she'd made for him for lunch untouched. His memory just wasn't the same anymore. She knew her mother's death two years ago had affected him. Lately, though, his appetite had disappeared. He was also more absent-minded. And yet, if she didn't know any better, she'd say he'd been gaining weight lately. Thank goodness she'd come back home to live. If it wasn't for her accident, she doubted she would have fully realized how much he needed her help.

She set about fixing soup to go along with the uneaten sandwich. After she called her father to the table and got him started on his meal, she escaped upstairs for her shower. She'd eat later, after the meeting.

Under the hot spray, her muscles slowly relaxed. Getting John Dalton's kitchen straightened had taken more out of her than she'd thought. Normally, when she first cleaned a new customer's kitchen, she expected to spend a couple of hours. This time it took twice as long.

In the future, however, her work in that kitchen would be minimal. She wondered if John would be blinded from the gleaming counters and appliances.

Dressed in a pair of gray cotton pants and

a cream-colored blouse, she grabbed her purse off the bed and went downstairs.

She entered the kitchen just in time to see her father putting his dirty dishes in the sink.

"Aren't you going to the meeting, Dad?"

"Yes, I'm going to take Betty. You go on ahead."

Marion frowned. She couldn't understand her father's attitude about the plans for the lot next door. He didn't seem bothered at all. She couldn't tell if he didn't understand the implications of what would happen once the city approved the plan, or if he just didn't care.

Well, she cared enough for both of them. This was her home too and she didn't want the intrusion of screaming kids and parents right next door.

In the car, she inserted the key in the ignition, then glanced up at the white clapboard two-story house. When she'd moved away five years ago, she never thought she'd be returning. A graduate of Georgia University, she'd taught school in Atlanta—third grade—and had loved every minute of it.

Until that fateful December afternoon when she'd been traveling on 285, the perimeter around Atlanta. It'd been raining all day. Then just as school let out, the rain turned to sleet. The car in front of her lost control, spinning, careening from lane to lane. In the end thirteen cars were involved; four people were dead. And she'd lost her ability to have children.

The doctors had told her she was lucky. At first they didn't think she'd be able to walk. She didn't feel lucky, even after she'd proved them wrong and was walking again in several months. But there was nothing she could do about her inability to have babies—she had the scars to prove it.

By the time she arrived at the courthouse for the commissioners' meeting, darkness had descended. Though it was the first of June, the humidity hadn't settled in for the summer yet. The bank display had read a cool seventy-five degrees when she'd driven past.

It appeared a lot of folks were interested in tonight's meeting. It took her several minutes before she found a parking space.

Inside the meeting room, Marion recognized several neighbors. She took a seat in the back of the room.

Just as the chairman pounded his gavel, she saw her father and Betty Carrington enter. They took a seat across the room from her.

"Quiet, please."

All conversation ceased and all eyes turned toward Jimmy Meyers, a man who had devoted his life to serving his community. With white hair, a slight paunch, and a deep, booming voice, to Marion he didn't look any different than he did years ago when she was a small girl.

"We've got an important agenda tonight. And judging from the size of this crowd, I suggest we get right to it. Last month a request was made for changes on the vacant lot on Red Maple Road. The floor is open for discussion."

One at a time, several of the more outspoken citizens spoke their views. Marion watched the reactions of the crowd. At this point, the crowd appeared divided. Some thought it was a good thing; others, like herself, were emphatically against it.

Then the chairman said, "Let's hear what the owner of the property has to say. Mr. Dalton?"

Marion's eyes widened. John Dalton, her newest client, was the man trying to change their neighborhood! She watched as he got up from his seat and moved to the front of the room. Even from this distance he appeared tall.

When he turned to face the crowd, she was surprised to see him wearing glasses. She didn't remember him wearing them earlier. He took them off, folded them, and stuffed them in his shirt pocket. Tonight he wore a tie, and though he now stood for everything she was against, she had to admit he looked decidedly handsome. He started talking about the area youth and how the world had changed for them and how they needed a place to play. His voice was steady, confident, and almost commanding.

She saw that some of the people whose mannerisms earlier had shown they were against the plans were now siding with him.

Betty stood up and asked for more specifics. Without hesitation, John spoke of benches, lights, even a concession stand with the profits going to maintain the field. He continued, "In fact, I'd like to turn a corner of the lot into a playground area with a couple of picnic tables, swings, seesaw, etc. for the younger children—an area for the grandchildren—"

Marion couldn't keep quiet any longer. She stood.

"Mr. Dalton." She saw the slight change

of his expression as he recognized her. "Those lights you're talking about will face my father's house, and will shine in his windows. What about the increased traffic, the noise, the litter? This is an old, established neighborhood. The people on this street have lived there for years. Many are retired. It's a nice quiet neighborhood and what you're proposing will change all that."

A crescendo of voices, echoing approval of her statement, rose. With satisfaction, she noted the surprised look on John Dalton's face. Jimmy pounded his gavel several times before the crowd quieted.

Mike Chester, one of the other commissioners, spoke. "Before this goes much further, I'd like to know what our city attorney has to say."

John sat down and Charles Turner stood up, turning around to face the crowd. At fifty-five, he still had a full head of hair, wavy and all gray. His deep tan came from the hours he spent in his boat fishing every weekend.

"What Mr. Dalton is proposing isn't for commercial use. It's a playground with the emphasis on baseball. To be honest, there are no real facilities for our kids to play ball. The field now in use, located right at the city limits, is leased. The lease expires in three months, and the owner is going to extend his pecan orchard. The city would have to find another location at that time, or do without.

"With budgets as tight as they are, the city hasn't been able to find suitable property as a replacement. In effect, Mr. Dalton has the city's approval; he isn't violating any zoning ordinance. But he also must have the approval of the nearby residents."

Even before Charles Turner could sit down, hands went up in the air, and everyone was talking at once. The chairman looked at his watch. He pounded his gavel. "It's obvious we're not going to settle this issue tonight."

Frank Dibble, the newest commissioner, spoke. "Mr. Chairman, I propose you appoint a committee to investigate this situation further. And I make the motion that we table this decision until next month."

Another commissioner seconded the motion. It passed. With that settled, Marion got up and left the room quietly, as there were other issues for the commissioners to consider that night. Several other people got up and left too. Normally, she would have stayed for the entire meeting, but she was tired. It'd been a long day and she still hadn't had any supper.

As she made her way home down the quiet streets, she felt satisfied for the moment. No decision for now was better than nothing.

At noon the next day, Marion pulled into the Pizza Hut parking lot. Stepping from the outside sun into the dim interior, she noted the place was busy for lunch—as usual. Peggy Lyman, her best friend since fifth grade, waved at her from a corner booth.

Marion made her way over to her. "Sorry I'm late," she said, sliding into the booth opposite Peggy. Where Marion was thin, Peggy was voluptuous, with generous curves, but she had to fight to keep from gaining weight. With long dark hair, she usually wore it in a long braid. When she appeared in court, the braid became a chignon at the nape of her neck for a more professional look.

"Business must be picking up. You look tired."

"I am." Not being able to get to sleep last night was the reason for the slight shadows under her eyes. She had John Dalton to blame for not getting to sleep.

"Ready to sign on with me?" Marion teased.

"And give up my partner? Not a chance."

"How is Rob?" Peggy and Rob had been high-school sweethearts. Both became lawyers and returned to Briar to practice.

"Good," Peggy replied.

A screech came from the booth behind Marion. Startled, she twisted her head around. A toddler, a little girl with soft brown curls, sat in a high chair, her arms reaching for her drink. Her mother held onto the cup while the little girl drank.

Turning back around, Marion tucked her hands under her thighs, sitting on them, and stared at the table.

"Marion?"

She looked up at Peggy, knowing full well that she couldn't hide anything from her best friend.

"It's been a year. You've got to accept—"

"How do you accept something you can't have, something I'd planned for since we were little girls? All I wanted was to be able to have a child of my own some day."

"Don't you think you need a husband first?"

"In this day and age?" Marion sighed. She brought her hands up to the table, folding them with the fingers intertwined. "No one's going to want damaged goods."

Peggy laughed. Marion scowled at her. "Good grief. I can't believe this is you talking. You make it sound like you're soiled. You've got a lot to offer a man."

"What about Seth?"

Now it was Peggy's turn to scowl. "Seth was a jerk. I tried telling that to you after you brought him here for Thanksgiving two years ago. He was obnoxious, boring, and he wasn't right for you."

"He said he loved me."

"If he loved you so much, where is he now? The fact he ran out on you after the accident, when it looked like you'd be in a wheelchair for the rest of your life—Well, I say if he really loved you, he would have stuck by you no matter what. It's his loss, not yours."

The waitress interrupted them, setting down the unsweetened tea Peggy had ordered for both of them.

Marion remembered the one and only visit Seth had made to the hospital. When she told him about her injuries, he blanched and stepped away. The moment he'd taken that step away from her, she knew what he was going to tell her. And he did. Their relationship was over. It had taken her nearly two months to stand, and another month of intense physical therapy before she walked without any telltale limps. He never called or saw her again.

"You're right." Marion sighed.

"But that doesn't mean all men are like that."

"Peggy, I'm just not interested in another relationship right now."

"When are you going to go back to teaching?"

"I'm not."

"Marion, you just can't ignore the past and waste your education like that. You loved teaching."

"Dad needs me."

"And what if he didn't? What would be your excuse then?"

Marion's eyes widened in surprise. Peggy leaned toward her, covering Marion's hands with her own. "You're my friend, my best friend, and I hate seeing you hurt like this. Your father doesn't need you taking care of him."

"You're wrong, Peggy. Yesterday he didn't even remember to eat lunch. He's done that a lot lately."

"He doesn't look sick to me. Why, he's one of the healthiest men around. Healthier than my Rob. Maybe there's another reason he has no appetite."

Marion didn't know what to say. She knew Peggy wasn't saying these things to be mean. Peggy cared.

"Just promise me one thing," Peggy said.

"What?"

"That you'll consider teaching again. You're good, and the system can't afford to lose you."

"And what if I did go back? You'd lose your cleaning lady." Peggy was her first and most devoted client. If it hadn't been for Peggy's praise in the right circles she would have had only a fraction of the customers she had now.

"Rob and I survived before."

Marion laughed. "That's what you called that chaos? Surviving?"

"Okay, so I'm not the world's best housekeeper. I bought the list of supplies you needed." It was Marion's policy to have her clients keep the necessary cleaning supplies on hand. When they needed replenishing, she left a list.

"Come on," Peggy said. "Let's go see what they're serving."

Marion followed her friend to the buffet table, selecting her pizza. Suddenly, she felt Peggy nudge her.

"Look what just came in the door. If I wasn't already married, I'd be interested."

Marion looked. It was John Dalton. Beside him was an attractive blonde. They looked good together, and without knowing why, it saddened Marion.

Collecting her silverware and napkin, Marion turned, intending to return to her seat. She had to wait for a family to pass by before she could move. By the time she got to her booth, with Peggy right behind her, John was being seated at the booth next to hers. He saw her.

He smiled, turned, and said something to the woman at his side. He grabbed her elbow and they both turned toward Marion.

Marion set her plate down and steeled herself. She wasn't sure what to expect, not after last night. Out of the corner of her eye, she noticed Peggy had set down her plate and was standing right smack behind her. Obviously, Peggy wanted to be introduced.

"Marion," John said, "I'd like you to meet the person who arranged for your services. This is my sister, Yvonne."

"I apologize for tricking you," Yvonne

said. "But my husband and I thought my baby brother needed a useful birthday present, rather than a tie or another pair of socks."

Marion immediately liked the woman. Her eyes were chocolate brown, similar to John's, and now that she knew this was his sister, she could see the resemblance.

"John's thirty now, and we thought it was about time he cleaned up his act," Yvonne continued.

John groaned. Yvonne grinned and Marion found herself smiling.

Turning sideways to include Peggy, Marion said, "This is Peggy Lyman, a great attorney if you ever need one, and my good friend."

Peggy, John, and Yvonne exchanged the usual words when introduced.

"We'll let you get back to your pizza now," John said. "I wouldn't want to be the cause of it getting cold."

"Happy Birthday, John," Marion said.

"Thank you."

Marion turned and sat down.

Peggy sat back in her seat and stared at her. "Well, well, well."

"What?" Marion picked up her fork and cut off a piece of pizza.

"You didn't tell me you knew Briar's most eligible bachelor."

"I don't."

"Didn't look that way to me."

"He's my newest client."

"And . . . ?"

And the man is trying to ruin our neighborhood, she wanted to say. Instead, she said, "*And* nothing." Marion didn't want to talk about John any more. He did things to her she didn't want to feel. She was still feeling the sting from Seth's hasty retreat.

Over the years, she and Peggy had discussed everything. There were no secrets between them. But suddenly she felt the need to change the subject. Marion asked about the house Peggy and Rob were building, and was grateful that the discussion for the remainder of the meal never came back to John.

All during lunch, however, she couldn't help but be conscious of her newest client. Though she tried to concentrate on what Peggy was saying, she kept hearing the low rumble of John's voice behind her. Whenever he laughed, the hair on the nape of her neck tickled, and every time she felt a shiver race through her, she knew John was looking her way.

Marion was relieved when Peggy looked at her watch, announcing she had to get back to work. They separated in the parking lot after Peggy looked over Marion's new van and gave her approval.

Driving to her next appointment, Marion tried to concentrate, mentally listing the errands she needed to run afterward, but her thoughts kept returning to John. Now that she knew he was the force behind the changes in the lot next door to her home, she was dreading Saturday. She'd managed to get through this meeting today, but Saturday could be different. And very confrontational. She could only hope he wouldn't be there.

Chapter Three

Marion rang John's doorbell, hoping he wouldn't answer. She didn't like the way he stayed in her thoughts. All she wanted to do today was clean his apartment—the quicker the better. No interruptions. No discussions. No accelerating heartbeats.

Though she always had the keys to her clients' houses, her habit was to knock first. She never knew when a client might be home. The last thing she wanted to do was embarrass them or herself by walking in.

Not expecting an answer since there was no car in the driveway, she waited another few seconds before opening the door.

She had imagined she'd find John's apartment messy, but the bedlam that greeted her when she stepped inside was shocking. Boxes and clothes were everywhere. The living room was a disaster. She'd never seen anything like it.

Picking up a pair of purple pants, she frowned at the size. They'd only fit a small boy, and a skinny one at that. A closer look revealed the clothes were a hodgepodge of sizes. There were baby clothes and women's clothes too.

She wondered if the rest of the apartment looked as bad. A quick look showed her the mess was contained in the living room. The rest of the rooms were untidy, but not nearly as bad as they had been Monday.

In the kitchen, she deposited her tote bag on one of the chairs, rolled up her sleeves, and opened the dishwasher. It appeared John hadn't unloaded it completely. From the looks of it, he'd taken dishes out of it as he needed them, then stacked them in the sink. Judging by the contents of the garbage, it also appeared John had brought home a lot of his meals. The bulk of his dirty dishes were coffee mugs and silverware.

Two hours later, she was folding towels and sheets at the kitchen table when she heard a key in the lock. A few seconds later she heard voices. Curious, she went to the living room.

"Oh, hi!" John said, seeing her in the doorway. He set the box he carried on top of another pile. Several boys, looking to be about eight or nine years old, held boxes in their arms too. "I'd forgotten you were going to be here."

"It *is* Saturday."

"You're right." To the boys, he said, "Just set them anywhere."

With a few grunts, they did, then looked to John, almost as if on cue, Marion thought. It was easy to see by the look in their eyes that they liked the man.

A freckled redhead spoke. "What time do you want us here tomorrow?"

"The earlier the better. It's a shame we've got to haul all this back out into the yard."

The boys grumbled their agreement.

"But hopefully by the time we're done, we'll have enough money to buy uniforms."

A chorus of "yea's" sounded. The boys headed for the door.

"See ya tomorrow, boys." John closed the door after them. To Marion, he said, "Sorry about the mess. We're holding a rummage sale. I'm trying to get the boys some uniforms, so we can play other communities this summer."

"Baseball uniforms? Does that mean you're already practicing?"

"Not yet. In a couple of weeks. But once we start practicing and playing we won't have time for the fund-raisers."

"Oh."

"I saw you at the meeting the other night. I'm sorry you're opposing my efforts."

"I don't oppose what you're doing with the boys—whatever capacity that may be. I just don't like having the lot next to my father's house made into a high-traffic zone." She went back to the kitchen to finish her tasks. As far as she was concerned, the subject was closed.

She could tell by the way John followed close behind her, however, that he didn't think so.

"What have you got against baseball?"

"Nothing."

"Then why are you opposing my creating a place for these boys to play? It gets them off the streets."

"I'm not opposed to your plans. I'm only against the particular lot you've chosen." Before, when she'd been in the kitchen alone, there'd been plenty of room to work.

Now, with John's large frame in the room, there seemed to be little space to move around.

"Why?"

"I explained why at the meeting."

"I want to hear your reasons again."

Marion hands stilled, and she looked up from her work. She hated that he stood there relaxed, leaning against the counter with his ankles crossed, and his arms crossed, which only emphasized how wide his chest and shoulders were.

"First, there's the litter."

"And what if I told you that the boys are planning to keep the lot clean? There's going to be a cleanup committee."

Marion smiled knowingly. She knew from her own experience that kids were enthusiastic in the beginning, but when the real work began, their energy ebbed and they needed constant prodding. She continued folding the laundry as she spoke. "Do you really expect boys of that age to follow through? It sounds good in theory, but...."

"There'd be adult supervision."

"Again, that's good in theory, but adults tend to back out too. All it takes is one adult not to show up, the kids to do a haphazard job, and the neighborhood will end up with trash in the yards."

"Why are you so pessimistic?"

"I'm not. I'm a realist."

"Sounds like you know kids well. How many do you have?"

"None." The minute she spoke she knew she sounded waspish. She wished she could retract the way she'd said it. The folding completed, she lifted the pile of laundry into her arms. "Excuse me. I've got to put these away."

Immediately, John straightened, his eyebrows in a frown. He grabbed the pile of towels and sheets from her. "I'll do that."

Their hands touched as he took the large pile from her. Her gaze flew to his, and she pulled her hand back fast and took a step back.

Feeling a bit flustered, but not wanting him to know it, she immediately turned, picked up the dishcloth and started wiping an already-clean counter.

"I'll be right back," she heard him say.

The swinging door swooshed closed, telling her she was alone. She took a deep breath and expelled it shakily. What was it about John that made her feel this way?

How could she be attracted to him when he stood for something she was against?

Her stomach growled, and she glanced at the clock. No wonder she was hungry, she thought. It was past lunchtime.

Retrieving her turkey submarine sandwich and her thermos of lemonade from the refrigerator, she sat at the table. Just as she took her first bite, John came through the door. The food stuck in her throat, but she made herself swallow. "Lunchtime," she said.

He eyed her sandwich appreciatively, then opened the refrigerator. She knew without looking what the contents were. A jar of pickles, mayonnaise, mustard, catsup, a few eggs, half a loaf of bread, and two slices of leftover Domino's pizza. And as far as she was concerned, the pizza was history—the edges were curling. His cupboards didn't fare much better when it came to food.

Pulling the bread out, he opened a cupboard and retrieved a jar of peanut butter. Grabbing a knife from the draining board, he sat across from her. "The staple of a bachelor. I try not to think of how many of these things I've eaten in my lifetime."

"You can have half of my sandwich," she said. "I made too much."

"I couldn't take your food."

"No, really." Before he could protest again, she slid half of the sandwich to him.

"It looks great." He eyed it again, then he picked it up and bit into it. "Mmmm. Pure ambrosia."

Marion smiled. He was practically purring.

"What's in it?" Lifting the edge of the bread, he peeked into it. "Tomatoes, lettuce, onion, pickles—"

"Salt, pepper, mayonnaise, and green pepper. It's easy to make."

"Easy for you to say. I can't cook. And when it comes to buying produce. . . . Well, I guess you could say I can't shop either. Is there some secret to buying fresh produce?" With his second bite the sandwich was already half gone.

"There are some tips that might help you. I've got to say, you don't look like you've been starving," she commented. He looked wonderful as far as she was concerned. Too wonderful. She had a hard time keeping her gaze off him. Her pulse picked up every time he was in the same room with her.

"No. Thanks to the local restaurants—in particular, the Colonel, Mickey D's, and the two nearby pizzerias—I stay fed."

"Are you saying you can't even make something as easy as this?"

"To me, that's not easy. I'd rather build a sixty-four-room martin house from scratch than build something this complicated."

Marion laughed. "This isn't complicated."

"It is when the knife takes on a life of its own. I go through a box of Band-Aids a week. I won't tell you how many times I've had to go to the emergency room because of that beast," he said, pointing to the stove. "In the emergency room my name is John Burn Dalton."

Laughter bubbled from Marion's throat. John laughed with her and by the time they both caught their breath, they were wiping tears from their eyes.

"You should laugh like that more often," John said. "It becomes you."

Her heart thumped erratically against her ribs. With all her heart she wished they weren't on opposing sides over this baseball park. She could really like him. "Are you serious about being able to build a martin house?"

"Yes. Haven't you noticed my balcony?"

"Not since the last time I was here."

"I've added something," he said. "Let me show you."

Marion followed him through the living room, to the sliding glass doors. When he drew the curtains open, she gasped in delight. About a dozen birds flew away—birds that had been dining on seeds in three different feeders fastened to the rail of the balcony. She didn't remember them being there before.

Even though John's apartment was on the second floor, there was a martin house, situated in the middle of the courtyard and almost level with his balcony. It was huge, and even had porch railings.

"The landlord let me put that up in the yard," he said, gesturing toward the martin house. "She enjoys birds herself and thought all the tenants would enjoy it."

Marion had to admit it was a wonderful idea. There were four apartment buildings, all with porches and balconies facing the courtyard. The martin house was located right smack in the middle of the yard. Every apartment had a wonderful view of it. She noticed other feeders on a few of the other balconies, and that they looked similar to John's.

"Did you make the feeders too?"

"Yup. I've got a list the length of my arm of people who want them."

"When do you find time to build them?"

"On rainy days. The boys help when they can. My landlord has a back room behind the office she lets us use. Her son is one of the boys on the team. It's another fund-raiser for us."

"Dad's always talked of building a martin house. Just never got around to doing it." An idea occurred to her. "Once a week I teach cooking at the high school. Would you be interested in a swap?"

John looked at her speculatively. "What kind?"

"I'll teach you to cook—at no cost—if you'll build a martin house for my father. Deal?"

He stuck out his hand. "Deal."

She rested her much-smaller hand in his. Immediately, her hand was enveloped in his warmth. She felt the calluses just below his fingers, and found herself squeezing his hand. He squeezed back in return and smiled.

"When's the first lesson, Teach?"

"Wednesday night, seven sharp."

"I'll be there."

They returned to the kitchen to finish their lunch. With his sandwich gone, he turned his chair around so he was leaning against the wall, his long legs spread out in front of him, the chair tilted back on the rear legs.

"You know, we never did finish our earlier conversation. Why are you against a baseball field for the town's kids?"

She was glad she'd just finished her sandwich too. Had he asked her this earlier, she probably wouldn't have been able to swallow one bite. "I'm not against it. I told you, I'm against your choice of locations."

"I know one of your objections is the litter. What else?"

"The lights. I'm assuming there will be night games; otherwise, aren't you restricted to playing after school and on weekends?"

"Not necessarily. During the summer, it's not dark until nine. And even though we're in south Georgia, we can't play throughout the winter, at least not when it's cold and raining. That could be weeks at a time or months at a time depending on the season we're having."

"Does that mean you won't install lights?"

"If it meant the difference between being able to get the field or not, then we'd schedule all games during the daylight hours. How does that sound?"

"Reasonable. But how about the noise? This is a neighborhood made up of elderly people, John. They nap during the day; they're set in their ways."

"Looks like you're the one set in your ways. You're young. Don't you think these retired folks would enjoy sitting on their porches watching the activity?"

"What about the added traffic going up and down the road?"

"I chose this lot because it's centrally located between two of the biggest elementary schools on either side of town. The roads aren't heavily traveled and the kids can ride their bikes there. The parents wouldn't have to drive the kids back and forth. Plus, many of these kids are from single-parent homes. Their mothers work and can't drive them anyway."

"Sounds like you've got all the answers."

"Got any better solutions?" He ran a hand through his hair. "Honestly, I'm trying to work this out. Frankly, I don't understand why you're so determined to see this project squashed."

"My reasons are my own. I care about the elderly folks in this area. Too many people want to take advantage of them."

"Is that what you think I'm doing?"

"I know you're trying to do something good for the young people, but it shouldn't be done at the expense of the elderly who live in the neighborhood." She paused. She didn't want this to turn into a confrontation. If that happened, she'd start to lose interest in her work here. "Look, I don't want to mix our politics with business. I have a job here in your home. If I believe you're going to question me every time I come, I guess I'll have to find a way to refund your money— your sister's money—after all."

John studied her for a moment. "You're right. I'm being unfair. No more talk about the lot unless we're on neutral territory."

Marion nodded her acceptance. "If you'll excuse me now, I've got another hour's worth of work. I've got another house to clean yet this afternoon."

"Right. Don't worry about the living room. I promise by next week the clothes and boxes will be gone. Whatever we don't sell is going to charity."

An hour later John looked up from his drafting board when he heard Marion at the door. He took off his glasses. "I'll see you Wednesday night. At the high school."

"See you Wednesday," she echoed.

Shutting the door behind her, she paused,

then stared at the door. John Dalton did nothing out of the ordinary, and yet it was as if she couldn't wait to get out of his apartment. She admitted she enjoyed having him around the apartment even if he did send her senses into orbit. She could still smell his after-shave that had lingered in the bathroom earlier. And seeing the wet towels, she'd automatically hung them up. Touching them had left her with a shaky feeling. It was ridiculous, actually, to feel that way, but she couldn't help it.

If anything, she'd made the whole situation worse for herself. Now she'd be seeing him Wednesday nights as well. Every Wednesday night. She didn't know whether to curse or count herself lucky.

Chapter Four

All day Wednesday, Marion thought about the cooking class she'd be teaching that night. And one new student in particular. As she spent the day cleaning, she found her normally well-organized methods defeating her. She kept forgetting things and found it took her twice as long to do even the simplest of tasks.

Later at home, she fixed dinner, but found she couldn't eat it. Her stomach had a field of butterflies in it. As she scraped her untouched food into the disposal, she was glad her father hadn't noticed how she'd pushed her food around. Though, come to think of it, by the looks of the food that remained on his plate, it appeared he didn't have much of an appetite either.

He sat at the table reading the paper. He didn't look ill, though, nor did he look unhappy. In fact, quite the opposite. Suddenly, it occurred to Marion that during the past few weeks her father had been whistling. The last time she heard him whistle was just before her mother got ill and then died.

Marion glanced at the clock. "Oh, my gosh! I've got to get going."

"Teaching tonight?" Joseph asked.

"Yes. Interested in coming?" She always invited him, but he always refused.

"No. I thought I'd pull a few weeds out in the garden since I've got another hour or so of daylight." Her father loved his flower beds and vegetable garden. The neighborhood benefited from his vegetables that grew in abundance. There was no way the two of them could eat all of that food. Whenever she could, she used the fresh produce in her cooking class, but even then there was more than they could use.

Ten minutes later, her clothes changed and her hair combed, she gave her father a kiss on the cheek as she passed him on her way out the door.

At the grocery store, Marion raced downed the aisles shopping for the rest of the ingredients she needed for tonight's class. But once she got in line to check out, she realized she was cutting it close, especially since everyone in front of her was writing out-of-town checks or purchasing items that needed a bag boy to go back and check on a price.

Pulling into the school parking lot, she wasn't surprised to see the cars of her students already parked. It wasn't often she arrived late. Usually, she was able to greet her students as they arrived, and they'd talk about the students' successes and failures during the past week.

Marion hated to be rushed. As she swung her legs from beneath the steering wheel, her nylons snagged on the keys. The nylon started to run. Marion grimaced but didn't have time to evaluate the damage. If it ran, it ran.

She hung the strap of her purse on her shoulder, opened the side door of her van and hefted one bag of groceries in her arm, then reached for the other bag, setting it on the ground so she could shut and lock the doors. Finished, she grabbed the bag on the ground, and felt it tear. Apples spilled onto the pavement, and her purse slid off her shoulder, hitting her sharply in the thigh. She wanted to scream, but instead gritted her teeth, and attempted to grab the apples that threatened to roll under her van.

"Need some help?"

Startled, Marion jumped, nearly dropping the grocery bag in her arm.

John Dalton rescued the bag, quickly taking it from her.

"You gave me a fright." She bent and with quick motions retrieved the apples.

"Sorry about that. Let me take that one too." He took the torn bag from her before she could protest. "I've been looking forward to tonight."

Marion glanced at him sharply. He was dressed casually in white cotton pants and a light blue, striped short-sleeve shirt. A slight breeze lifted the hair off his forehead lightly. He smiled at her and his eyes twinkled. He looked like an eager student on the first day of school. Obviously, she had read more into his words than he'd meant. He'd already admitted he couldn't cook. That was the only reason he was eager for tonight to arrive. No other reason. For her to think otherwise was foolish on her part, she berated herself.

Upon entering her classroom, she was dismayed to see everyone was waiting for her. Never feeling clumsy as she prepared her dishes, tonight she felt like the biggest klutz of all time. She tried to tell herself it had nothing to do with the man who hadn't left her side, but she knew he was totally responsible for the fact she couldn't even toss the salad without leaves of lettuce spilling on the countertop.

Unlike other cooking instructors, she preferred not to use an overhead mirror and keep her students in chairs. She encouraged them to stand around the counter and asked for their help throughout the evening. At the moment, John was stirring the Alfredo sauce. She smiled at the way he peered into the pot, stirring the contents slowly, his glasses slipping down his nose, watching as if he were waiting for some miraculous event.

"Stir it just a little bit faster, so the bottom won't burn," Martha, a young pregnant woman, instructed him.

He did. The level of the sauce started to rise. "What's happening?!"

Marion chuckled. "It's just bubbling up. Turn down the heat. Keep stirring," she told him. "It's not cooling fast enough. Lift the pan off the burner for a minute. Keep stirring."

She watched as he followed her instructions. It always amazed her how panicky her students got when something unusual happened.

"How do I know when it's done?" John asked.

Before Marion could answer, Walter, a young man about to enter college, did. "What do the instructions say?" Walter looked at Marion with an apologetic expression. "Oops, I'm sorry."

"No, no," Marion said. "This isn't a class where there's just one teacher. We're here to help one another. Often when cooking, you need teamwork, assistance from family members or guests. You're all doing well. And you were right, Walter." Turning to John, she repeated the student's words. "What do the instructions say, John? Whenever in doubt, read."

John picked up the foil wrapper, and started to read. His eyebrows knitted together. It was cute the way he studied the instructions.

"Don't stop stirring while you're reading," she reminded him. She asked another student if the noodles were ready. They were. Everyone was waiting on John now.

"It says to stir about five minutes until thickened," he finally said. Once again he peered at the concoction. "Is it thickened?"

"What do you think?"

He shrugged his shoulders. Theodore Tilley, an elderly man whose wife had died recently, spoke up. "I've learned it helps to watch the time."

John looked sheepish. "I guess I forgot."

"Don't worry," Marion told him. "At first, you'll need to time your cooking. Once you become familiar with how the food should look when it's done, you'll soon be able to judge when something's done."

"Looks done now," Joan, a young mother of twins, pronounced. "Let's eat!"

Everyone laughed. When Marion first started her cooking class she found the highlight of the evening was when the students got to taste their achievements. The students were harder on themselves when it came to declaring the dish a dismal failure or a gratifying success. After the food was gone, the dishes were washed and put away, and the classroom put back in order, all in quick time.

Marion locked up and followed her students out to the parking lot. As she approached her van, everyone was pulling away except John. He leaned against his car, and she had to pass him to get to her vehicle.

Marion's footsteps slowed, but her heartbeat accelerated. He'd been waiting for her intentionally, and she wasn't sure if she wanted to know why or not.

"After a scrumptious meal like that, there's only one thing to do." John pushed off and stepped toward her.

With anxious eyes, she watched him come closer. Tonight his eyes reminded her of warm chocolate syrup, and she felt her cautious nature soften. She'd had fun tonight, more than usual, and John was responsible. Though he was the most inexperienced in the class, his quick humor made the time fly swiftly.

"I think a sundae is called for," he said.

Marion found herself grinning. "We did forget dessert, didn't we?"

"What's your preference? Strawberry, chocolate, caramel?"

"Hot fudge."

"Ah, a connoisseur if I ever saw one. A purist. Your taste buds are of the most exquisite—"

Marion laughed. "You must like hot fudge too." She said it as a statement of fact, rather than a question. From the way he'd carried on, she had an inkling he'd been about to pronounce his own good taste.

John's face appeared crestfallen. "How did you know?"

An emotion that had become a stranger to Marion—pure enjoyment—bubbled up within her.

Marion agreed to meet John at the Dairy Queen; it was silly for him to bring her back to the school. Fifteen minutes later she dug her spoon into the soft-serve ice cream, then scooped the spoon into the hot fudge.

"If there's a heaven, surely hot-fudge sundaes are a part of it," John said, licking his lips.

Marion agreed. "I couldn't help notice, the staff here knows you by name and didn't even ask what you wanted."

"I'm a regular. When I come in here this time of night, they know I'm after my hot-fudge sundae. I told you I depended on the restaurants around here, but now that I've got the secret of a wilted salad and Alfredo sauce under my belt, well, they won't be seeing me anymore," he boasted.

"Ah, I don't think you want to burn your

bridges—or rather, your food supply—quite yet."

"In other words, I've still got a lot to learn."

"Whenever I start a class, I ask my students what their expectations are, what dishes they like and want to prepare. You're coming into this class a few weeks after everyone else. What are your expectations? Do you have any favorites dishes?"

"I like the standard steak and potato. I know how to use the grill, but even then my steak tastes bland compared to a restaurant's. And I've given up on the potato. Everyone talks about how easy it is to use a microwave, but I don't think so. My potatoes either explode or are as hard as a rock."

"It's not as difficult to use the microwave as you think. First of all, did you read the instructions and cookbook that came with the microwave?"

"Well . . . not really. And then when I tried looking for them—"

"Let me guess. You couldn't find them."

"I guess I'm not very organized."

"It's not just a matter of being organized. If you don't read the instructions, you're bound to fail. You need to have a plan and stick to it. Take your baseball, for instance. What would happen if the bases were changed every time a game was played?"

"There'd be confusion." He grinned sheepishly. "Kind of like when I don't put things back where they belong?"

"You go to the head of the class. Actually, there's nothing complicated about a microwave. For a while, you need to stand close by while you're using it and check your food every fifteen or thirty seconds—"

"Fifteen or thirty seconds! I was checking it every five minutes."

Marion laughed. "No wonder your potatoes exploded. Plus, I bet you don't pierce them."

John scrunched up his face. "I've got to pierce my food? Sounds like we're regressing to the caveman era."

She couldn't help but laugh again. "No, it's nothing like that. I'll see if I can't find a simple microwave cookbook and leave it with you Saturday when I come. Do you have a library card?"

"Sure."

"Give me your number and I'll check a few cookbooks out for you. For homework," she said.

"Homework. You didn't tell me there'd be homework."

"There's always homework. You won't learn unless you make some mistakes at home."

"I've made enough mistakes to last me a lifetime."

"Just think—if you study the books I get you and try to use something out of them every day, in a relatively short time you'll be cooking meals at home you never thought you could. How is it that you never learned to cook? Not that you're untypical these days—a lot of people these days, both men and women, don't know how to cook."

"That's true. I guess the days of the traditional homemaker, the wife with the husband supporting the family, are gone. As a family, we were all on the run. Rarely did we sit down to eat together. We were always busy doing something. Our meals consisted of hamburgers and hot dogs. Bowls of chili in the winter. And soups. My mother always claimed if it wasn't for Betty, the Kids, and the Mrs., we would all have starved."

"Betty, the Kids, and the Mrs.?"

"Betty Crocker, the Campbell kids, and Mrs. Paul."

Marion laughed. "What activities was your family involved with?"

"A lot of different things. Mother's a librarian, always involved in story hour and projects for the children, and my father's a professor. He's definitely the clichéd absentminded professor. My mother always claimed she could have put Styrofoam pellets on his plate and he'd say it was a great casserole. They both love the outdoors. We were always camping, hiking, bicycling, playing tennis or golf, and we all played softball in the summer. I guess that's where my love of the sport, all sports, comes from."

At the mention of softball, Marion remembered the lot next door to her dad's and wondered how she could have forgotten about it. What was it about John that made her ignore their differences? At least during the time she spent with him. Right now she didn't feel at odds with John, but she couldn't let that feeling get in the way of what John was trying to do to the property next door.

Yet at the same time, she realized how much she missed being able to talk to someone like this. It wasn't the same when she talked with Peggy or her father. Though she was close to them, it just wasn't the same as sharing a conversation with someone you loved— What a mistaken thought that was. For her to think she was in love with John was ridiculous. She barely knew the man.

Though she was still hurt and angered at what Seth had done, leaving her the way he did, she had always enjoyed their conversation. It was that feeling she experienced now. She didn't want to think of her future as an old maid, a spinster, being remembered as the woman who never married. Before, she had never considered that one day she could be denied a husband and a family. These days, however, it was all she thought about. Everything was different now.

Determined not to think about her past and her dismal future, Marion turned her attention back to John. "Tell me about your childhood," she said. "Do you have any brothers or sisters?" Their ice cream gone, the empty plastic cups sat in the middle of the table, discarded.

John's eyes sparkled as he talked. Marion was reminded once again how much his eyes were like the color of the hot fudge they had just eaten. "I have an older brother and two younger sisters," he said. "Mark is married, an attorney about to become a justice in the juvenile court system in Atlanta. You've met Yvonne. She lives in Thomasville. My other sister lives in Nashville. She writes music, and sells pianos and guitars. She hasn't found anyone to record her music, but she plays it whenever she demonstrates the pianos and guitars. I've got to give her credit—a lot of her customers ask where they can find the music. She's gone ahead and made it into sheet music, not waiting for someone else to produce it for her."

"Do you see them often?" Marion asked.

"Not often enough. We get together every summer and at Christmas. Mom and Dad still live in North Carolina, where we grew up. It's hard for us to get together more often than that."

"What brought you to Briar, of all places?"

"I went to college at Florida State University and my roommate was from Moultrie. Since I didn't have the opportunity to go home very often, Greg was always bringing me home with him. We had to drive through Briar every time, and I fell in love with the community. I loved the old Victorian houses. I remember one spring vacation we drove through Briar and the whole community appeared to be one big flowering garden. It was easy to see that the people cared about their community, and I thought it would be a great place to live. Plus I saw they were building a new elementary school. I was hoping there would be a need for teachers as I was going to be graduating that summer. On the way back, I stopped and picked up an application. I've been here ever since—seven years now."

"You teach? But I thought—"

"That I was a cartoonist? I do both. I prefer to think of myself as an artist first, a teacher second—not that I'm slighting the profession. But I knew how difficult it was to make a living as a cartoonist. Until I break into syndication, I'll remain a teacher."

He was a teacher. She hadn't a clue, and yet it explained why he was so comfortable around kids. It also made her a bit wary. If he knew she'd once been a teacher, he'd wonder why she had quit. Though she wanted to change the subject, at the same time she was curious. Curiosity won. "What grade do you teach?" she asked.

"Believe it or not, I'm the art teacher. I teach all grades in the elementary schools."

"That's not hard to believe, given your

cartooning. But what an eclectic combination—an art teacher and coach."

"Plus I teach seventh and eighth grade health. It's the 'dreaded' class. Frankly, I love it. I remember how difficult that age was for me so, consequently, I can relate to the kids. I was lucky. I had understanding parents who eased me through the transition of puberty with relatively little pain or embarrassment. It's my hope I can do the same for these kids. It's harder these days, for both the parents and the kids, and it disturbs me the way we throw away the kids, the relationship, or whatever else it is that's wrong. We don't take the time to make things right."

"Isn't that sharp criticism considering you've never been married or—"

"Or had any kids? I suppose. I guess that makes me an idealist. I like to think any problem can be worked out as long as we're willing to talk about it."

Was that how he saw her? Unwilling to talk? She had to admit her feelings about the property next to her father's house were pretty strong. But then so were John's.

He continued. "I guess that's why I got involved in the city's baseball program. Every summer as I was growing up, we took off for picnics, parks, museums, anything that caught our interest. The kids around here don't have access to those activities, not unless they're driven or bused. Baseball is one of the few outlets they have.

"One day, shortly after I'd gotten settled in, I happened to stop at the playground and watched some kids playing ball. One kid— he could only have been about eight or so— asked if I knew anything about the game. Before I knew it, we had set up teams and I was coaching them.

"None of us knew how late it was until some mothers came looking for the youngsters. When the kids asked if I'd be there the next day, how could I refuse?"

Marion remembered all too well how easy it had been to get involved in the activities of the children she had taught. In a way she missed it.

"Why don't you come out and watch us sometime?" John suggested.

Marion's gaze flew to his. "No," she said. "I couldn't do that."

"Have you got something against baseball?"

"No, not at all."

"Then you must have something against kids."

"No." She stared at a water spot on the table. Suddenly, she felt chilled. Goose bumps appeared on her arms. She wanted to believe the ice cream was responsible, but she knew that wasn't the case at all. John's effect on her was downright disturbing. So was their conversation.

"Come on," John coaxed. "We need an umpire. We need an unbiased umpire. Or so the kids tell me."

"I . . . I wouldn't make a good umpire."

She darted a glance at John. She could tell he was puzzled by her refusal to come watch him. Actually, she wanted to watch him. She just didn't think she was ready for . . . she just wasn't ready for that.

Marion didn't want to protest too much about not wanting to go. She knew if she dug in her heels John would start to wonder, maybe even question her more. She tried to focus the conversation elsewhere. Anywhere but on her. "Where do you play ball right now?" she asked.

"At the school yard at North Elementary."

Just then a man and his wife stopped and said hello to John. He introduced her to them, then Marion listened politely as they talked for a few moments. It was obvious that the two were teachers and knew John well.

After they left Marion asked, "Is he a coach too?"

"Yes. High-school football. He's really worried about the team this year."

"Why?"

"Too many players were struggling academically this spring. If it continues this fall, we won't have a team. They won't make the grade average needed to play."

Marion sighed. She knew what a problem it was for some kids to get good grades. All too often she'd had her share of students who needed nothing more than a few hours of extra tutoring or someone who could help them along. Unfortunately, when kids like these slipped through the cracks and ended up with a diploma though unable to read or perform math, it hurt everyone—the community and the student. The strength of a community, whether a small town, city, or a country, rested on the education of its citizens.

John collected their refuse and slid out of the booth. She followed him out the door and then to her car.

Opening the door for her, he said,

"Thanks for the company, Marion. I enjoyed the conversation."

He kissed her lightly on the lips, then turned and walked toward his car. Marion put a finger to her lips, still feeling the slight sensation. It was nothing. Just a friendly thank-you. All she'd done was ask a few questions. He'd done most of the talking.

It was just as well. She wasn't comfortable talking about herself these days. She sighed, wondering if she ever would be again. Though she had to admit, she had opened up to John more than she had anyone else—other than her father and Peggy—since returning to Briar.

Chapter Five

Marion arrived at John's mid-afternoon Tuesday just as he was leaving. He carried a duffel bag and the handles of several bats stuck out of the bag at one end, making it impossible for it to be zipped completely.

"Wish us luck," he said. "We're playing Cairo today. They're good. They've been together as a team for several years."

She wished him luck and watched him drive off. If his kids were half as excited about the game as he was, they were sure to win.

Marion spent the rest of the afternoon cleaning John's apartment, and as she was ready to leave, the doorbell rang. Answering the door, Marion received a telegram for John. Knowing he was at North Elementary for the game, she decided to take it to him. For someone to send him a telegram, it had to be important.

Minutes later, Marion turned into the school parking lot. Unable to find a space, she parked on the grass. The humid air settled on her once she left the cool, air-conditioned interior of the car. The afternoon was sweltering. She heard yelling and cheering. As she approached the corner of the school, the noise got louder.

Going around the building, she saw the playground. There weren't any benches, so spectators had brought blankets and lawn chairs and were watching from the sidelines. Immediately, she saw John. He was coaching, yelling to the boy who had just passed second base. John was motioning him with his arm to continue past third and go for home.

She looked for the ball and saw an outfielder pick it up and throw it just short of the second baseman. Everyone was yelling now, some parents standing, duplicating the motions John made. As the boy rounded third, the noise became deafening. The second baseman picked up the ball and the catcher stepped up to home plate to catch it.

Now everyone was on their feet. The second baseman threw the ball as the runner was halfway between third base and home. The noise of the crowd—both spectators and participants—became a roar. The runner dived for the base as the catcher caught the ball, then stuck out his hand in an attempt to tag the runner.

To Marion it looked like a dead tie, with the runner at the base the same time he was tagged.

Then the umpire made the call. Safe.

John grinned from ear to ear and the boys on the team—the winning team—jumped up and down, shouting with glee. John stepped into their midst, said a few words, and then the boys, as one unit, turned toward the other team and moved toward them. Solemnly, they shook hands with the boys they'd just beaten. The parents and other spectators packed up their belongings.

Marion made her way toward John. When he spotted her, she saw his eyes widen in surprise.

"Congratulations," she said when she was

finally at his side. "It was a glorious victory."

"Wasn't it though? I didn't think it was going to happen. We were down ten to one after the seventh inning."

"Just goes to show what a little determination and a good coach can do."

"Isn't he the best?"

A youngster about nine years old, with sandy brown hair and the biggest brown eyes Marion had ever seen, stood nearby. Though a large quantity of freckles dotted his nose and cheeks, it was easy to see that he would grow out of them and turn into a handsome young man. He'd never have a problem finding a date. And it was obvious that he worshiped John.

"Look, Coach! There's a fight."

Marion and John both looked to where the boy pointed. Near home plate two boys were pushing each other. All the parents were gone. Only a few boys remained, and they were around the two boys who were fighting.

"Ah, excuse me," John said. "I've got a problem to take care of."

"That's Joe and Bobby," the boy said. "They're best friends. They fight sometimes too." He cocked his head at Marion. "Do you belong to the coach?"

Startled, Marion's gaze flew back to the boy. "No. I . . . ah . . . work for him."

"Oh. I thought you might be his girlfriend or something."

Marion watched John again. The fight was over and he'd made all but the two boys involved move on. He spoke to them in a quiet tone; she couldn't hear anything, only saw his lips move. Then the two boys shook hands. Marion smiled. John would make a wonderful father.

The thought left her with a hollow feeling.

"What's your name?"

Again, the boy beside her demanded she give her full attention to him.

"Marion. What's yours?" He was a cute youngster. He reminded her of her own students she'd had in her class, the way they had looked at her sometimes while they waited to hear something wonderful, new, and exciting. Such a wondrous age. She wondered if this boy's mother knew how special this kid was—or if any of the mothers who'd been here earlier knew how precious their children were. How lucky they were to have these kids.

"Billy Warren."

She noticed he looked fairly clean, lacking the dust and dirt the other kids had collected on their skin and clothes. "Were you playing today?"

"Not today," Billy said. "I just got over the flu and Mom thought it'd be best if I didn't run. But that doesn't mean I can't bat. Are you our mascot?"

Marion laughed. "No, I don't believe so. Are you going to have a mascot?"

"Coach said we were going to get one. What's a mascot?"

Marion smiled at Billy's innocence. "A mascot is usually an animal. A dog, a goat."

"Gee! I wonder what kind of mascot we'll have. Are you someone's mother?"

Her smile disappeared. "No." Would the pain never stop?

Just then a woman's voice called out to Billy.

"I gotta go," he said. "That's my mom."

Marion watched as Billy ran up to his mother, who stood at the corner of the school. The woman waved at John and he waved back.

"You were so emphatic about not coming today, what brings you here?" John asked as he approached Marion. "Whatever the reason, I'm surprised. Delighted, actually."

She held up the telegram. "This came for you. I thought it might be important."

"Oh," he said. A bit of the sparkle left his eyes. She wondered whether the disappointed look was because it took a telegram to bring her out here, or whether he expected the telegram to be bad news. Now she wished she had commented on the game before telling him about the telegram. It was a good game, what little she'd seen of it.

He took the telegram from her and opened it.

"I hope it isn't bad news," she said.

Reading it, John laughed. "No, it isn't. It's Yvonne's way of being cute. She always did have a flair for the dramatic. She's pregnant."

"Oh." A lump formed in her throat. "You're going to be an uncle."

"For the first time. I know the folks will be happy. She was the first of us to get married. Last summer. I guess I'll have to call her when I get home. Are you all right, Marion? You look pale."

"No . . . nothing is wrong. Actually, I need to get back to work."

"Are you sure you're all right? You just don't look well all of a sudden."

"No, I'm fine," she insisted. She had to stop feeling so sensitive every time something like this happened. Sooner or later she had to fully accept what had happened to her. All her life, from her childhood when she played with dolls to her late teens when she mentally collected the names that she would give a daughter or a son, she'd planned on motherhood.

Even now she shuddered at the thought of attending a baby shower or helping out at the church nursery. She couldn't face it. If she couldn't have children, why should she have to deal with other people's children? It wasn't fair. She knew John was worried about her right now. But she didn't know what to say to relieve his concern.

"It's been a long week," she finally said. "I guess the heat is getting to me." She thought it a weak excuse, but John seemed to accept it.

"Thanks for bringing me the telegram."

Though he smiled, Marion thought the smile didn't quite reach his eyes. He was still looking at her with concern.

"You're welcome." She turned and walked away, knowing John watched her. She also knew he had questions that she couldn't explain. Not yet. Even though she could talk about her problem with Peggy, she wasn't ready to share it with anybody else. She didn't want to see the pitying look or hear the comforting words.

The rest of the week crawled by for Marion. At night she couldn't get to sleep. And then when she did sleep, she kept dreaming of John. During her waking hours she spent useless energy trying not to think about him. The more she tried not to think about him, the more she did.

When she went to his apartment Saturday and the following Tuesday, he was gone. Actually, there was very little for her to do. Either he was cleaning up after himself, or he hadn't been spending much time here.

The following night, she found herself looking for him at the cooking class and was strangely disappointed when he didn't show up. All during the rest of the week, the radio irritated her with its crooning love ballads.

Even her father was acting differently. He was busier than normal, spending a lot of time with Betty Carrington across the street. At one point, he told Marion that Betty needed help cleaning out the garage.

Marion kept expecting to see stuff taken to the curb or taken to the dump, but she didn't see much activity, let alone progress, made with Betty's garage. To Marion's way of thinking, the garage and its contents hadn't changed at all.

Though she was concerned about her father, she felt she shouldn't intrude. He was happy, so she left him alone. She wished, however, that she could feel as happy as he did.

Everywhere she went she heard kids. In the grocery store, on the street. She became conscious of every pregnant woman she saw. Marion knew she was feeling envious. Sadly, she wondered if she'd ever heal the wound that stayed raw within her.

Friday night, arriving home tired and even more depressed than when she'd left that morning, she decided she needed a change of scenery. With John's apartment the only one to clean tomorrow, she packed a bag, intending to travel to the Gulf afterward and spend the rest of the day at the beach, soaking up the sunshine.

The next day, however, dawned dreary, wet, and stormy. Determined not to let the weather get her down, hoping it would clear by the time she finished her work, she went ahead and threw the beach bag into the van along with her regular supplies.

As usual, she knocked on John's door and had her key in the lock, when the door opened.

Surprised, she said, "Oh, you're here." He wore well-faded blue jeans and a baby-blue v-neck cotton pullover shirt. And he looked thoroughly pleased to see her. Her heart skipped a beat.

"We were supposed to have our first game of the season, but Mother Nature decided to have her say. I'll try to stay out of your way."

Marion entered the apartment, not understanding her nervousness. John had been here before when she worked. Why was she more nervous today?

She knew why. She was attracted to John. And though she'd denied it until now, she wanted him to be attracted to her. Another dream that would never happen, she thought gloomily.

As she moved from room to room, she noticed he worked diligently over his worktable in the corner of the living room. He kept brushing back a stray lock of hair, his concentration never deviating from his work.

At one point, Marion stood at the door, debating if she should disturb him by asking if he wanted lunch. For a moment, she watched as he worked the pencil across the page, how he cocked his head, then squinted at his work with a critical eye. Then once again, he bent over his work, the pencil moving again.

No, she'd go ahead and fix a sandwich for both of them. But first she wanted to finish cleaning up the bathroom. As she worked, she hummed. Music was a great remedy for a gray day.

The job done in quick order, she stored the cleaning supplies back under the sink.

Finished, she rose and saw John's image in the mirror.

"You should hum more often," he said. "It's a nice sound."

"I didn't want to turn on the radio and disturb you."

"I doubt I would have heard it. I tend to bury myself in my work."

"I noticed. But you did hear me humming."

"No, I got hungry. I can make a mean grilled cheese if you're interested in lunch. Is it possible to earn extra credit or impress my teacher?" He grinned and the dimple on the left side of his mouth became pronounced.

For the first time that day, Marion felt the oppressive mood she'd been fighting all week start to lift. She was tired of struggling against what she felt for John. She didn't want to see him as the enemy, the opposition, anymore today. He was reaching out to her and she wanted to connect. If nothing else, she just wanted to enjoy his company.

"Sure," she said. "But the extra credit? I'd have to consider that request carefully. I wouldn't want it known to the other students that I'm a pushover for grilled cheese sandwiches."

"Don't worry. Your secret will be safe with me."

Marion wondered exactly how safe she was with him. He made her laugh so easily. And despite their differences, she wanted to be in his company. She loved the way his eyes crinkled when he smiled. And his smile was contagious; she always found herself responding. Right now, as she watched him slather the bread with butter and drop it into the hot pan where it sizzled, she couldn't even remember feeling depressed this past week.

The next hour passed quickly. Too quickly. They'd eaten and the kitchen was clean again. Marion was pleased to see that John had purchased the staples she'd suggested to the class last Wednesday, giving them a list. She'd explained that with these supplies on hand, there were any number of simple meals that could be made better with just a few added fresh foods, spices, or condiments.

"How about a game of Monopoly?" John asked.

Surprised at the invitation, Marion wasn't sure what to say.

"It doesn't look like the rain is going to let up," he said, looking out the sliding glass doors. It was true. It was as if the heavens were squeezing every drop out of the skies all at once. "Or maybe you had other plans."

"Not anymore," she admitted. "I'd planned to go to the beach, but it doesn't look like I'll be going now."

"Well, then, I'd say a challenging game of money management is in order. Or don't you believe you can beat me?" he dared. She noticed the grin he tried to squash.

For the first time in a long time she wasn't looking forward to going home. She knew her father would be taking a nap by this time. Or he'd be across the street with Betty. She didn't want to go home to a quiet house with the afternoon stretching ahead of her. "You're on," she said.

Actually, she liked the idea of beating him. The corners of her mouth lifted as she looked forward to him begging for a loan as he paid her high rents.

"Just to make it interesting," he said, "let's deal a third hand. That way some properties can never be developed."

Four hours later, she groaned as she landed on Park Place.

"Oh, oh." With his tongue bumping his cheek out as he tried not to laugh at her plight, he appeared to study the card that would determine her rent.

"I don't understand it!" She moaned. "An hour ago you only had five bucks to your name and the only property you owned was Boardwalk."

"I bet you realize now that you were foolish to give me Park Place."

"What!? You left me no choice! It was that or mortgage all my houses. I still don't understand how you manage to sneak past my whole street of hotels every time around the board. Do you have a leprechaun or something in your pocket?"

"Must be," John said.

Marion stood, stretching, as John picked up the board and dumped all the playing pieces into the box and found the lid. Taking a glance out the glass doors to see if it'd stopped raining, she noticed a rainbow. "John, look."

She went to the window. The sun sent down a shaft of light in the distance. The faint rainbow she'd spotted became brighter in color. As quickly as the rainbow appeared, it disappeared and it started raining again, harder than ever. She turned, prepared to leave. Instead, she turned and stumbled against John. He'd come up behind her and she hadn't heard him.

He grabbed her to keep her from tumbling. She glanced up at him and their gazes locked. Her heart thumped wildly. This close, she could see golden flecks of color in his brown eyes.

They were close enough to kiss, she thought. Her gaze dropped to his mouth. She wondered what it would be like to kiss him. A true kiss. Not one just between friends.

He took a step back and his hands dropped from her arms. Disappointment filled her that he wasn't going to kiss her after all.

"Thanks for ... for the afternoon," she said.

"You're welcome. Since I took all your earthly possessions, I feel it's only right that I offer you dinner."

"Lunch and dinner, all in one day. I'm impressed."

John grinned. "Don't be. I was thinking in terms of Pizza Hut."

Marion knew she should refuse. It wasn't wise to encourage him. Nothing good could come out of a relationship with John. Instead of turning him down, however, she said, "I'd like that."

"Do you want to go now or would you like to change?"

Marion looked down at her usual wardrobe of jeans and a T-shirt. In winter she substituted a sweatshirt for the T-shirt. "I think I'd prefer to change."

"Okay. I'll pick you up in say, fifteen minutes?"

"Half an hour. I want to check on Dad." Actually, she wanted to wash her hair. Even if she was just going to a local restaurant, it wasn't every night that she had an opportunity to go out with the town's most eligible bachelor.

Chapter Six

Twenty-five minutes later, she set down the blow-dryer. Since cropping her hair short to ear level, then layering the thickness a bit to give height, Marion had found the new style easy to care for. Her hair was now curled without the aid of gels and mousse. Wondering if she should add some shadow to her eyes, she quickly decided no. She didn't want it to look like she had fussed too much. Mascara and lip gloss were her standard fare. It would have to do for tonight.

Glancing again at her outfit, she was glad she'd splurged earlier in the week and bought the white knit short-sleeved top with a light pink-and-blue design.

Her gaze rose to the face in the mirror. She'd always thought her blue eyes were a tad too far apart. But she was content with her looks. Though she wished her cheeks weren't quite so pink tonight. She couldn't help feeling this was more like a date than a consolation for losing a game of Monopoly. Maybe that explained the high color in her face and the way her eyes shone back at her.

Hearing the doorbell, she turned off the light and scampered down the stairs, exclaiming loud enough so her father would hear that she had the door. Opening it, she found herself a little breathless.

Seeing John didn't help. He looked fabulous. He too had changed. His yellow cotton shirt and light brown Dockers only emphasized the warmth in his brown eyes that were inspecting her as thoroughly as she did him. She could tell by the light in his eyes that he approved. The fact that she wanted him to approve wasn't a good sign, she cautioned.

"Let me tell Dad I'm leaving." She heard her father walking toward them. "Dad, can I bring you back anything?"

"No, no, I'm fine," he said, coming to the door. He stuck out his hand. "Hi, I'm Joseph Winter."

"John Dalton."

"So you're the young fellow determined to turn the lot next door into a baseball diamond."

"Yes, sir, I am."

"I want to talk to you about that sometime."

"Any time you say. Just call me. I'm in the phone book."

Before the conversation could go any further, Marion grabbed her purse and went out onto the porch, hoping John would follow. She didn't want any discussion of the property to mar what had been an otherwise perfect day. John followed her, but only after the two men had shaken hands again.

In the car, she watched as John walked around to his side. She knew her father well enough to know that he'd follow through and have his talk with John. She wondered what her father would say. She hoped John wouldn't feel too bad, once he realized there was no future for the ball field.

On the short trip to the restaurant, John told her he had informed several of his friends, some married, some not, about her service and that most of them were inter-ested. From the way John talked, it sounded like she could plan on her business dou-bling. If that was true, she'd be hiring help a lot faster than she had anticipated.

Considering it was Saturday night, Mar-ion expected the pizza parlor to be busy and it was. They had to wait a few moments for a booth. Finally, they were seated. Quite easily, they agreed on a taco pizza and in seconds the waitress was back with their sweet tea.

Suddenly Marion felt tongue-tied. She glanced around, noticing the other patrons. At one large table, a group of teenagers—both boys and girls—were teasing and being playful. In a corner booth an elderly couple, eating their pizza, never looked at each other.

"You know, I always thought it was sad seeing a couple like that."

John's gaze followed hers. "Maybe they're so comfortable with each other they don't need to talk," he said.

Just then several small boys raced by. One tripped and fell next to their booth. Marion gasped and started to move. But even before she could slip across the seat, John was already there, picking the boy up and setting him upright on his feet again. The boy appeared dazed, as if he wasn't quite sure what had happened.

"Are you all right, son?"

The youngster nodded, then grinned, revealing a gaping hole where he'd lost two teeth.

He looked so adorable, and yet so mischievous, Marion found herself grinning. She could tell the boy was anxious to get back to his friends.

"Yes, sir," the boy lisped. "I'm fine." Then he scampered off.

For the first time in a long time, Marion realized she wasn't cringing at seeing a child. True, Marion couldn't change her own plight, but she couldn't stay away from children for the rest of her life either.

Peggy was right. It was time to deal with her problem, not continue to avoid it. She had to accept the fact that she'd never be able to have children, that she'd never have a family. She could live with it... eventually. What choice did she have?

All too quickly, the evening passed with John talking again about his family. She enjoyed listening to John talk about his brother and sisters and of their adventures growing up. Being an only child, she'd missed those kinds of adventures. At one point she said, "I'd like to meet them sometime." She meant it.

Now she watched as John circled the front of the car and opened her door. She took his proffered hand and hoped he wouldn't feel her pulse skipping erratically.

She had thoroughly enjoyed the day, their playing, talking, and sharing, but realized their friendship was still fragile. She had a long way to go before she would feel safe confiding all her secrets to him.

As they walked up the steps, she prayed that John wouldn't expect the usual goodnight kiss, but on the other hand, she knew she'd be disappointed if he didn't kiss her. She hated this seesaw of ambiguity she was on.

For her, the day had been pure enjoyment, a time to relax. She wondered now, however, if she was the only one that felt that way.

It was so hard to tell what John was thinking.

John put a hand on her waist. Marion tensed. Swallowing heavily, she turned to him, and glanced at him briefly.

Before she could say or do anything, he

kissed her lightly on the forehead and had already moved down the steps.

"John?"

He stopped, one foot on the sidewalk, the other on the last step. Pivoting slightly, he turned to her.

The last thing she expected to see was his slight grin.

"Thanks for today. I had a great time."

His smile broadened. "So did I, princess. So did I."

Finally, after what felt like an eternity but was in reality probably only a few seconds, he added, "Sleep tight."

Then he was in his car, and she watched as the taillights of his car disappeared.

Marion sighed, clutching her handbag to her chest. Melancholy filled her. Determined, however, not to let her thoughts take root or to fantasize about something that couldn't be, she pushed open the door.

She dropped her purse on the table in the hall and paused, listening. The house sounded quiet.

"Dad?"

Silence.

Walking into the living room, Marion expected to find her father asleep in front of the television, but the screen was dark. A search of the house revealed her father was gone. She frowned when she didn't find a note. Where could he be?

Marion went back onto the front porch. Maybe he had gone for a walk. She looked up and down the street but didn't see him. Then she heard Betty Carrington's door opening. Marion wasn't surprised to see her father leaving Betty's, considering how often he was over there. But then she saw them kiss.

Not wanting them to spot her, she stepped into the shadows. This wasn't the usual neighborly peck on the cheek, but rather a kiss that could be construed as passionate. Realizing her mouth had dropped open, she snapped her jaw shut.

Everything made sense now. The time they spent together. Obviously, they were sharing a number of meals; no wonder her father wasn't as hungry as she thought he should be. It had never occurred to her that her father might want to date. Nor had she ever imagined him kissing another woman for that matter. Actually, even when her mother was alive, it'd been years since she'd seen her parents kiss.

Quietly, Marion shut the door. She didn't want to embarrass her father.

A few minutes later, he found her in the kitchen unloading the dishwasher.

"How was your evening?" he asked her.

"Good. How was yours?" She glanced at him and saw the beaming smile on his face.

"Ah . . . it was good."

Marion wasn't sure what to say now. She didn't want to intrude on his privacy, but at the same time she wondered if maybe she was in his way just by living with him again.

"Dad, I was thinking. I'm going to start looking for an apartment of my own."

"Why in the world would you want to do that?"

"I . . . well. . . . "

"What is it? You can tell me."

"It isn't so much that anything's wrong with me." Once again she heard herself hesitating. There was no easy way to say this. "I saw you with Betty a few minutes ago."

Their gazes met and Marion saw that her father understood what she was trying to say.

"Oh," he said. "I guess I should have said something, but I wasn't sure how you'd take the news. She lost her husband a year before your mother died. What with your mother's death two years ago.... " His voice trailed off.

"Dad, you deserve to be happy. I mean, while it's true I never thought of you being with someone else.... " This time it was her turn not to finish the sentence. She didn't quite know what to say.

Her father spoke instead. "I like Betty. A lot. I didn't mean to keep our relationship from you. After your mother's death, I became the neighborhood handyman."

"I noticed." Marion grinned. His services were needed by the other elderly around here—especially the women—and got him out of the house and forced him to spend time with other people. And because he was good at what he did, his services were in high demand.

"The more time Betty and I spent together, the closer we became. I usually go over there for lunch several times a week."

"Is that why I come home and find your lunch uneaten?"

Sheepishly, he answered, "Yes."

"I wondered why you didn't appear to be losing any weight. And here I thought your appetite was lousy."

"Can you forgive an old man for deceiving you?"

"You know I'd forgive you anything. As long as you're happy, Dad, I'm happy for you. Betty's a nice lady."

"I'd like to start dating her openly. What do you think?"

Marion draped the dish towel she was holding on the oven handle, then went to her father and hugged him. "Dad, you don't need my approval. But if that's what you're asking for, you have it. I miss Mom, but she's gone. Life is for the living, you know."

"I'm glad to hear you say that."

Marion kissed him on the cheek, then stepped back.

He wagged a finger at her. "For a smart cookie, it sure is taking you a long time."

Was he implying that she should follow her own advice?

"Really, Dad. If you want, I can find a place of my own. You and Betty might want some privacy."

"Nonsense. This is your home too. Besides, if we want privacy, we can always go to her house. She has no other family."

"She doesn't? I guess I never realized. She moved here after I left, didn't she?"

"Yes, right after her husband retired."

Marion hugged her father again. "Be happy, Dad." It was advice so easy to give, so hard to live.

Several weeks passed and she didn't see John whenever she cleaned his apartment. Nor did he attend her class. In another two weeks her contract with him would expire. She wondered if he was finished with her classes too. He had only attended four or five so far. And judging from his earlier enthusiasm at learning how to cook new dishes, she was surprised he'd missed so many of the classes.

It was Wednesday night again, and all the students had left. She slung her purse on her shoulder, gathered up her box of supplies, and turned off the light. Heavy footsteps sounded in the hall. Marion frowned when she realized the person was headed her way. Was one of her students returning, having forgotten something?

Marion peeked around the corner just in case it was someone who shouldn't be in the building this time of night.

It was John.

He spotted her and waved. She straightened and headed toward him. When they met, he took the box from her but kept a hand at her elbow as he propelled her outside. "Sorry I haven't been in class. Because of the rainy weather, we've had to reschedule some of our games. They've all been on Wednesday, and always ran into overtime."

"That means the team is doing well."

"Absolutely. Tonight, though, I had to attend a special dinner celebration. Remember Billy? The day you brought that telegram out to me?"

"Sure, I remember Billy. Cute kid."

"His adoption was finalized today. He wanted me as one of his godparents."

"Billy is adopted? I had no idea. He called that woman who picked him up that day mom."

"Officially, she is now." John peered into the box, moving a few things around. "Any leftovers tonight?"

"Sorry."

"Darn. I guess I was hoping I'd get here in time to sample."

"Usually, there are a few leftovers. But not tonight."

"I probably shouldn't ask, but what was the entrée?"

"Beef Stroganoff."

John groaned hungrily, and Marion

laughed. "You make it sound like you haven't had any dinner."

John's expression was pained. "Billy made up the menu. Hot dogs, french fries, and chocolate cake. I used to love hot dogs. But now they bite back at me." Marion chuckled. "So I only had one," he confessed. "The cake was great, though. When do we learn to bake something like that?"

"I suppose I could plan a cake for next week."

"Are you sure I can't convince you to tutor me in beef Stroganoff?"

"No, but I'll give you the recipes you've missed and the instructions."

"Then can I ask you for another favor instead?"

Puzzled, she wondered what he would ask.

"I know this is last minute, but I've got a class reunion coming up this weekend. I wasn't going, but apparently my sister thought I was. She's made arrangements to have the family get together because she's announcing her engagement and she wants the family to meet her fiancé. My brother will be there with his wife. So will Yvonne and her husband. What I'm asking is, would you be willing to go with me to Raleigh and attend the class reunion as my date? We'd be staying at my parents'. It's a big rambling house, and the more people who are in it, the happier my mother is."

Marion was flattered that he'd asked, but at the same time she didn't feel comfortable spending the weekend with him even though she'd be staying with his parents. She didn't like how her attraction for him was growing and felt that being with him for that length of time wasn't wise. In fact, it would make it that much harder for her to keep cleaning his apartment if anything went wrong. "No. I don't think that I can."

"I wouldn't ask this of you if it wasn't so important."

"Important in what way?"

"I suppose it's really petty, but you see, I've been told my old girlfriend is going to be there. To make a long story short, she dumped me shortly after high school. We went together all through high school. When I didn't go straight to college and started traveling around the country with no career in mind, she said I was turning out to be a bum. I had invited her to go along with me but she didn't want to. I soon learned how materialistic she was—she wanted power, money, and all the good things in life that accompany them. Less than a year later, she married a man twenty years older than her, someone who already had a family. Four children, I heard. I guess I don't want to go back to the reunion as a has-been. Although I haven't made a great success of my life, I'm happy and I'm content. That's all that matters to me."

"Then why should it matter if I go with you?" she asked.

"You're right. Frankly, I saw you as a barrier between me and the barracudas. I'm not interested in dating any of the women up there. I know from experience—from the last class reunion—that all the divorcées and single ladies latch on to any of the guys that are still single. I hear I'm one of the last bachelors of the class. To these gals I'll be a conquest. I just want to go and have a good time. I don't want to spend the entire evening defending my single status. But you're right. I should face it alone. If I can't do it, I shouldn't be going at all."

Marion considered what he was asking of her. It wasn't like he was asking her to go as his real date. Rather, he was asking her to accompany him as a friend. It would be nice to get away for a while. She hadn't left

Briar since she'd returned home after her accident. And she could use a vacation.

She also knew what John was talking about. She'd received plenty of pitying looks, having to answer questions she didn't want to answer. And when she didn't answer their questions, she knew she appeared rude and hard. She knew quite clearly the horrors of being observed, analyzed, and talked about. She wouldn't wish the experience on her worst enemy if she had one.

"I'll go with you," she said. "The drive up there will be nice. And it shouldn't be nearly this hot. We *are* driving, aren't we?"

"Yes, I thought we would leave Friday morning. That would put us up there mid-to-late afternoon."

That night as she lay in bed, Marion thought about her life since the accident. Before the accident, she was content with her life. Now she was restless. Thankfully, her energy level was finally back to where it had been before the accident. For another, she wanted a challenge. Her business was doing okay, but it wasn't enough. She wanted something more.

Suddenly, Billy came to mind. She remembered that he was adopted. Stunned at her next thought, she sat up in bed wishing it weren't nearly midnight but rather the middle of the day so she could put the thought into action. The more she thought about her idea, the more excited she became wondering why she hadn't thought of it before.

Settling back down under the sheet, she thumped her pillow, determined that sleep wouldn't evade her tonight. She wanted tomorrow to arrive as quickly as possible.

Chapter Seven

The next morning Marion drove to Thomasville. Nervously, she stood on the sidewalk in front of the adoption agency. What she was about to do was a big step. It would change her future. Taking a deep breath, she reached for the door handle, then grinned, realizing for the first time in a long time, she was taking a positive step for her future.

Moments later she was shaking hands with Stephanie Morris, the administrator of the agency. After they'd exchanged a few pleasantries, Stephanie posed her first probing question. Marion had expected tough questions, but not quite so soon.

"Why do you want to adopt?" Stephanie asked. Seeing Marion's hesitation, the caseworker hurried on. "Don't think I'm asking these questions just to be nosy. These are questions you'll have to answer on the questionnaire."

"Because I can't have any children of my own."

"How does your husband feel about this?"

"I'm not married. Will that be a problem?"

"That you're single? No. There's quite a number of single people that are adopting these days. But it is a consideration. I'll be honest. When it comes to placing a child in the home of a couple or a single parent, and there is no other obvious difference between the two families, the child almost always goes to the couple."

"That's understandable," Marion said. She knew from her own experience in working with young children that a stable family life with two parents was the best for a child.

"Where do you work?" Stephanie asked.

"I'm self-employed. I own a cleaning business. A maid service. Maid Marion. I started it about a year ago."

"Oh."

"That doesn't sound like a good oh."

"Let me ask you this. Do you have any other marketable skills? Not that owning a business is bad," Stephanie hurried on. "It's just that it's a fairly new business. I imagine you're still growing, that your income barely meets your expenses."

"That's true."

"And you're probably working long hours. Do you have any other employees? Besides yourself?"

"No."

"Believe me, Marion, I'm not trying to be critical. I just want you to be aware of what the adoption board will ask of you. Considering the hours you're working, who will take care of the child?"

"I want to raise this child. I was a teacher before the accident."

Stephanie looked at her notes, lay down her pencil, and said, "Marion, I'll be honest with you. This agency has nothing against a single parent. I think you'll be a wonderful mother. But for the child's sake, we have to be sure the child will be adequately provided for. The fact is . . . well, if you were teaching—a secure position within the community—it would go a long way in providing the kind of stability we're looking for."

"Yes, I can see that."

"Do you still want to go forward with this? Or would you rather I wait a few weeks before filling out this application?"

Marion mulled over what Stephanie was telling her. She could go ahead and process the application, but the outcome would be risky. Or she could plan and make sure the outcome would be in her favor. She decided to wait.

Planning for a child was a big step, one she wanted to take, but one she wanted to do right as well.

"Thank you, Stephanie. For everything. And for your honesty." Marion picked up the application, saying, "I'll be back."

Stephanie smiled. "I hope you will. We need more parents like you."

Knowing her father wouldn't be home yet, and needing someone to talk to, Marion stopped by Peggy's office.

She had barely crossed the threshold to Peggy's office when Peggy said, "All right, give. What's going on?"

"Peggy, I swear there must be some gypsy blood in your background somewhere. I'm always amazed at your clairvoyance."

"Stop flattering me and tell me your news. Don't make me suffer, or are you into torturing your best friend? That smile of yours is wicked. It must be something really good."

Marion sank into a chair. "It is. I'm going to adopt."

Peggy squealed, jumped up, came around her desk and hugged her close friend. "Ooh, I'm so happy for you. When?"

"Not right away. I've got to change a few things in my life first."

Peggy sprawled in the opposite chair. "Like what? Get married?"

"No." The question stung. Marion wished more than anything that she was telling Peggy she had plans to get married. She wondered if there'd ever come a time when she would be making those plans. "Nothing like that," Marion said. "Single people are acceptable as adoptive parents. It's my line of work, or rather my business, that's the problem. It's too unstable, too new. I've decided to go back to teaching."

"You're just going to give up the business?"

"No. I'll still do it on weekends, that or hire someone to do the actual work. During summers I can help out, allowing my employees time off if they want it. Listen to me. I'm going to have employees!" Even though this had been Marion's goal, she still couldn't believe it was happening so soon.

"I can't tell you how happy I am to see you finally move on with your life. I'm so excited for you. You really had me worried."

"I know. I can't believe it took me this long either. But what's past is past."

"So what's your next step?"

"Get hired as a teacher."

"With your skills and the demand for good elementary school teachers, that shouldn't be a problem."

"I want to teach in the high school."

"Are you crazy? Why? Do you have any idea what hormones do to those kids?"

Marion laughed. "I want the challenge. Plus I want to help those kids that are getting lost in the cracks. Not that high school kids have the market on getting lost in the cracks, but this is their last chance. I just want to do something different."

Peggy shook her head. "You always manage to surprise me. What does your dad say?"

"I haven't told him yet."

"What about John? Are you going to tell him?"

"No. It's not like we're going out or anything."

"But you're spending a lot of time with him."

"So, I spend a lot of time with you too, but that doesn't mean you and I are getting married."

"You know what I mean."

"There's nothing between us."

"Not that you wouldn't like it," Peggy probed. "I think you're skirting around the real issue here. You've fallen in love with him. You have, haven't you?"

Marion debated whether she should be honest with Peggy or not. Honesty prevailed. It had never done any good to keep any secrets from Peggy in the past. If anything, Peggy was her conscience. The last year had proven that. She'd be eternally grateful to her friend for pushing and prodding her into accepting her fate, and then doing something about it—even if Marion hadn't welcomed the advice at the time.

"Yes, I have."

"You should tell him."

"No."

Peggy started to say something more, but noticed the way Marion's eyes were scrunched up. It was a sign Peggy had come to respect.

At this point, Marion was glad she hadn't

told Peggy of her weekend plans. She didn't want her friend to make a mountain out of a molehill—and Peggy would do just that if she knew.

"All right, already. I'll stop. So when are you going to apply for the job?"

"As soon as I leave here, which is right now." She scooped the strap of her purse onto her shoulder and got up.

Peggy rose too. "You know I wish you luck." She gave Marion another quick, tight hug. "Let me know how it turns out."

"I will. Thanks, Peggy . . . for everything."

Peggy smiled. "You're welcome. Anytime."

As Marion drove to the school she considered all the changes that were taking place in her life: her father's new romance, her own new relationship with John and the fact that it wasn't going anywhere, her appointment with the adoption agency. Even, begrudgingly, John's softball program. Not that she begrudged him the program. Just the location.

If only she could just get John to agree to put his baseball field elsewhere, everything would be perfect.

*   *   *

It was late by the time Marion arrived home that night.

Her father was sitting in his favorite chair—a recliner that was older than she was. She plopped down on the sofa.

"Hi, Dad. What are you watching?"

With the remote control, he clicked the television off. "Just an old *Matlock* rerun. How's my favorite girl?"

"Great. I had an interesting day. I've got a new job."

"You do? I thought you liked your business."

"I do. But it's not enough right now. Actually, I've got lots of news. But first things first. I want to adopt a child and I went to the adoption agency this morning. Though there's nothing wrong with the business, it just isn't stable enough to provide an adequate income for me to support a child. I want to stack the deck in my favor, Dad. So I went to the high school, and starting this fall I'll be teaching high school English. I'm going to place my emphasis on reading— whatever it takes so more of our graduates are literate when they receive their diplomas. Plus I'm going to do a little tutoring here and there."

"Sounds like you're going to have your

hands full. But you look happy. Are you sure this is what you want to do?"

"More sure than I've been of anything in my life, Dad."

"Then there's nothing more to be said. As long as you've thought it through and it's what you want, that's all that matters."

"I'm going to be gone this weekend." She told him about John's class reunion. "What are your plans for the weekend?"

He grinned at her. "It's just as well that you'll be gone."

"Dad, if I didn't know better, I'd say you've got something up your sleeve."

"I don't know why you'd think that," he said with a gleam in his eye.

"Or should I say who? What's going on? Or isn't it any of my business?"

"No, I don't mind telling you. Betty and I thought we'd spend a day at Wakulla Springs, south of Tallahassee. Eat lunch and take a ride on their glass-bottomed boats. Spend the day in the park. From there we're going to the beach—Panama City. She's never been there."

"That's great, Dad. She'll enjoy it. Looks like we're both going to be gone for the weekend."

Her father winked at her. "And I can hardly wait."

Marion, however, wasn't sure how she felt about the coming weekend. As much as she was excited, she was equally nervous.

Friday dawned hot and hazy. The forecast on the radio called for a record-breaking scorcher of a day. Slipping on her knee-length jade shirtdress with the culotte skirt, she mentally checked off the items she'd packed in her overnight bag to make sure she hadn't forgotten anything.

A glance at the clock told her she was ready right on time. The doorbell rang and minutes later they were on their way.

The day and the miles sped by quickly as they talked about music, politics, and the plight of the environment.

As they got closer to Raleigh, John pointed out landmarks.

Marion liked the neighborhood they were driving through now. There was something intimate about the old houses and small yards that were filled with flower gardens. Up ahead kids were playing ball in the street, people sat on their porches talking, and young parents were pushing strollers down the sidewalks.

She sighed. She was impatient to implement her plans for adoption. At least she had a plan, and one day soon she'd have a child. Then, she could become part of the picture she was seeing now in front of her—a parent pushing a stroller. Or a parent teaching her five-year-old how to ride a bike.

For the moment, however, she'd have to be satisfied with her life. Right now her plans were still a dream. But, at least now, most of her dreams were within reach. The only thing missing was a husband.

Marion peeked a glance at John and caught him looking at her. Shyly she smiled and watched as he grinned broadly. She felt a catch in her heart and with a lurch realized she was falling in love with him. Swallowing the lump in her throat, she quickly turned her head pretending to look at the yards passing by. Instead, all she saw was a blur of grass, brick, and cement.

Regardless of anything she felt, the purpose of this trip was to help John out at his class reunion. Nothing more. She couldn't let her emotions complicate things, no matter how much she wanted a complete family.

John turned the car into a driveway. The house stood on a hill, the yard terraced and neatly groomed. The front porch, graced with six colonial columns, was wide with several rockers and a swing.

Seconds later, adults young and old spilled out of the house. Eagerly, John got out and embraced his mother, then his father. After that she wasn't sure who was who, as there seemed to be more people than could possibly be his siblings. Quickly, Marion discovered there were in-laws and friends here as well.

Not forgetting his manners, John reached out a hand to her. Reluctant to make it look like they were more than friends, Marion hesitated about taking his hand. But before she could do anything, John made the decision for her, grabbed her hand, and pulled her into the circle of his family, tucking her under his arm.

"Everyone, this is Marion. My housekeeper, teacher, and all-around good friend."

Waves of relief filled her, and she relaxed as she met his family.

Half an hour later, she was drinking lemonade and eating coffee cake at the huge table that filled the dining room. It was obvious that the family had spent a great deal of time around this table. The walls were covered with photographs of John and his brother and sisters, reflecting the various stages of their youth. There were pictures of weddings and graduations, baby pictures, and one of John when he was about seven years old holding up a fish bigger than he was.

She immediately liked Christina, John's youngest sister, and her fiancé, but at the same time Marion envied Christina's future. George, a backup singer for a popular country star who hoped to be recording his own music soon, was marrying into a wonderful, warm family. It was easy to see that Christina and George were madly in love.

That night as Marion lay in what used to be John's bed and bedroom, she gazed at the ceiling wondering if she'd done the right thing in coming here.

It wasn't that she was having an awful time. Quite the opposite. Throughout the evening she'd found her gaze constantly upon John, watching him interact with his family. And it was obvious that he cared a great deal about his family. Not once had she felt like an outsider.

A sigh of regret escaped her lips knowing she'd never have a family like that of her own. She had finally managed to hurdle the childlessness dilemma. But to expect a man—a man capable of having children—

to want to father someone else's child, was asking a lot. It would be too much to expect to get her child *and* a loving husband.

Despite that thought, she continued to think about what it might be like to have that loving husband.

Someone like John.

Shifting to her side, she punched the pillow, reminding herself not to get lost in her dreams, and not to read anything into John's words and actions. He was her friend. Hadn't he said as much?

Chapter Eight

The next day passed quickly as John took her sight-seeing to his old haunts—his elementary school, the big maple tree his very first girlfriend and he had hid behind where they shared their first kiss, the movie theater where he and his friends used to sit in the balcony and throw popcorn at the girls below, and the drugstore where he'd held his first job.

Later, they spent an enjoyable hour at a park playground on the seesaw and swings talking about their childhoods.

Marion had enjoyed the day immensely.

Now they were on their way to John's class reunion.

"Are you nervous?" she asked him.

"Naturally. Are you?"

"Not at all."

"Then why have you been smoothing out your dress ever since we got into the car?" He grinned at her.

Marion stilled her hands. Guiltily, she realized she *was* nervous. She had no idea what the evening would bring. As much as she had looked forward to being with John, acting the part of his girlfriend, she also dreaded it. The more time she spent with him, the harder it was to hide her feelings from him.

"All right. I'm nervous," she finally admitted. Unable to stop herself, she smoothed an unseen wrinkle from her skirt. "I'm afraid everyone will find out I'm a fraud."

John placed a hand over hers, giving her as long a serious look as he could before returning his gaze to his driving. "You aren't any more of a fraud than I am. If I haven't told you before, I'm glad you came home with me. It wouldn't have been the same."

Just then she saw the high school, recognizing it from their earlier outing. Cars filled the parking lot. When John opened her door, he held out his hand. She took it and was surprised when he didn't move aside after she'd stepped out.

He stood facing her, looking down at her. "I mean it. I'm very glad you're here with me tonight." He kissed her lightly on the lips, then draped her hand on his bent arm, leading her to the gymnasium. "And you look beautiful. You should wear white more often."

Tonight she felt beautiful. The dress was a favorite. Soft material resembling lace hugged her curves, before flowering into a full skirt. The short capped sleeves and sweetheart neckline felt light, allowing what little breeze there was to cool her skin. The skirt whispered around her legs as she walked. A simple strand of pearls at her throat and a pair of studs her parents had given her for Christmas one year were her only adornments.

Just before it was their turn to register, John grabbed her hand.

"Now *I'm* nervous," he said.

She let out a shaky breath and gave a little laugh.

He bent so his mouth was just inches from her ear and spoke in a low tone so no one else could hear him. "Why don't we skip this joint and go see a good movie?"

Marion turned her head sharply to look at him. Surely, he was kidding. Before she could say anything, someone else made the decision for them.

"Johnny!"

Both she and John turned. A towering bald-headed man clapped John on the back. Marion read his name tag. *Jason Buchanan.* He was one of the friends John had grown up with. Marion grinned, watching the two men greet each other. John introduced her and Jason shook her hand with his huge hand.

"You've got yourself a pretty one here, John. Hope you're keeping an eye on her. Someone just might steal her away from you."

John hugged her to his side. "No chance of that."

Marion smiled, warmed by the praise, but then she quickly reminded herself it was all an act. An act for the benefit of John's class-mates. But it felt so real. If only....

No, she couldn't second-guess John. Nor was he one to pretend. His emotions, his words, his actions were always genuine, which was making tonight so complicated.

Granted, the weekend had forced them together more, but nothing he'd said or done so far could be construed as the actions of a man in love. As she gazed at John's animated face as he talked with his friend, she reminded herself that she was here as his friend. Nothing more. Nothing less.

Once they were registered and properly tagged with a name badge, John led her to another group and introduced her. At no time did she feel like an outsider. There were a number of wives and girlfriends and once they found out about her cleaning service, they were asking for tips to make their work easier or more efficient.

The dinner buffet was set out shortly after that, and she and John got in line. It tickled her to see John sample each dish, and then determine the ingredients.

Throughout the meal, conversation flowed around Marion, and she noticed those who talked to John about his work with kids were impressed with what he did. Several times he caught her looking at him and each time he winked broadly at her, then grinned. And each time she found herself grinning back at him as if they shared a great secret. He had worried unnecessarily about the reunion—he was a great success, not at all a has-been.

Though John hadn't said anything about the old girlfriend, Marion had to wonder if the woman was even here. She'd noticed how John had looked around the room when they'd first arrived, and then appeared to relax. Obviously, the old flame wasn't here after all.

Once the buffet was cleared away, the band started playing again. John set her glass of tea down, and held out his hand to her.

"Dance with me?"

Placing her hand in his, she let him pull her up out of her chair, fully conscious of the slight pressure of his hand on her back as he walked behind her to the dance floor. She turned to face him, and his arms held her protectively yet firmly for the slow Righteous Brothers ballad the band played.

At that moment, as John propelled her around the floor, Marion realized more than ever that this was the man she wanted to marry. The ache in her heart, knowing it would never happen, swelled to giant proportions, threatening to overcome her. Determined not to let her feelings overwhelm her, Marion pushed her love for John back into a hidden corner of her heart.

John held her closer, humming the ballad softly as he guided her around the floor. And then, John pulled back so he could look down at her, and said. "I like you, Marion Winter, and I'd like to know you better."

Was it possible? She bit her lip nervously, and felt her heart accelerate. Was there a chance after all?

Daringly, she tilted her head back and gazed at him. He smiled warmly. "I'd like that too."

A painted fingernail tapped John's shoulder from behind him, and a small voice said, "John, is that you?"

When John turned, Marion saw a petite, curvy blonde with the biggest blue eyes she'd ever seen. A bright flash of jewel on her hand revealed a big, three-carat diamond ring. Marion suddenly felt dowdy next to this woman who was a Barbie doll come to life. Her designer dress was pure silk in a lemon yellow. With her deep suntan and long curling blond hair scooped up on the sides with tortoiseshell combs, no woman could compete.

"It *is* you!" The woman tilted her head up, encircled an arm around John's neck, pulling him down smoothly, and kissed him soundly. Marion noticed that John's facial expression seemed frozen, plus his movements were wooden.

John straightened, freeing himself from the woman's embrace. "Brenda."

"Johnny, where did you disappear to?"

"I live in Briar."

"Do I know Briar?"

"I doubt it. It's a small farming community in the middle of nowhere."

Brenda wrinkled her nose. "What are you doing in Briar?"

"I'm a commercial artist."

Brenda's face brightened. "Oh, you do commercials," she gushed.

"No, it's artwork for businesses. Freelance work for brochures, ad copy, and magazine and newspaper cartoons."

"What cartoon in the Sunday funnies is that? Although I don't read the Sunday funnies," she added, resting her hand on his arm. Marion noticed Brenda didn't remove her hand, and a few seconds later John lowered his arm and stepped back a little.

"I do political cartoons." He pulled Marion to him. "Marion, honey, I'd like you to meet Brenda."

"Hello, Brenda."

"Hello." Brenda gave Marion the briefest of smiles, barely looking at her. Her attention was immediately back to John. Before she could say anything, however, John spoke instead. "Marion and I are engaged."

Marion blinked, looking up at him. Had she heard him right? His hand gripped her waist tighter, pulling her even closer to him. She felt his thigh against hers, and he looked down at her with the same kind of expression she'd seen on the faces of her girlfriends' husbands. Like a man in love.

Was it true? Could he be in love with her, as she was with him? Though she'd been shocked at the way he'd announced their engagement—of all people, in front of his old girlfriend—

She'd been so caught up in the words and the soft touch that she'd forgotten the very reason why she was here. It was all an act. Still, just the thought of being engaged to John sent shivers up and down her arms. It was all for Brenda. None of it was true.

Marion smiled brightly at Brenda. "John's told me a lot about you."

"Oh." Brenda paused, then scrunched up her nose again as she gaped at Marion. For a few seconds Marion knew exactly how a bug under a microscope felt. Finally,

Brenda remarked, "It's been nice seeing you, Johnny."

Both Marion and John watched as Brenda approached another class reunion attender with her bright plastic smile and animated conversation.

"It was Brenda, wasn't it?" Marion asked. It didn't bother her that Brenda had snubbed her. From what John had told her about Brenda, she would have been surprised had Brenda not snubbed her.

"Yup. And I can't tell you how relieved I am right at this moment to know I avoided making the worst mistake of my life."

"And what's that?"

"I had wanted her back so badly after she dumped me, that I almost chased after her. I was ready to get on my knees and plead for her to take me back."

Marion looked at him incredulously. "You would do that?"

"Back then I might have. Not anymore. I believe in talking things out. After that, if your problems can't be worked out, at least you can part with dignity."

"What is she looking for?" Marion asked. Brenda spent only a few minutes with each person, not seeing the pitying looks sent her way.

"Someone worthy of her gushing. Someone who will ooh and ahh in all the right places."

"What about her husbands?"

"Rumor has it they disappear never to be seen again."

Marion looked up at John, then laughed, seeing that he was teasing her.

"Actually, I heard her husband left her. I'm lucky she let me get away when I did."

Silently, Marion agreed.

"You know," John continued, "I look at her now and wonder what I saw in her back then."

"What is it that any young boy sees in a girl other than good looks, a dimpled smile, and a curvaceous body," Marion said. "I bet she was a cheerleader."

"Actually, age has nothing to do with a man appreciating a beautiful woman, a gorgeous smile, and a great sense of humor."

Marion blushed beneath his stare.

He added, "And a curvaceous body isn't anything to be ignored either." His eyebrows worked up and down in exaggeration. "To answer your question, yes, she was a cheerleader. Enough about Brenda. I'd rather talk about us. Thanks for letting me use you to get me out of a jam."

"You were never in a jam."

"No? Then why did it feel so sticky there for a few minutes?"

"Must have been your imagination. I thought it went rather smoothly. And that was the reason why I came."

"You're right. I had almost forgotten that. Though I never expected us to be 'engaged'. I hope you're not angry with me for that. Can I make it up to you?"

"No, I'm not angry." If anything, she'd been elated, if only for a few minutes. "But how do you propose to make it up to me?"

"First, by dancing with you."

The way John looked at her was enough to make her melt into a puddle right in front of him. "I'd love to," she said softly.

The soft lights and the people around them became a blur of color as they circled the dance floor.

At one point, John leaned back and looked down at her. "Any chance you'd reconsider your policy about dating your clients?"

Marion's heart skipped a beat. "I shouldn't, you know."

"The world is full of should's and could's. You wouldn't want to be responsible for breaking my heart, would you?"

"No," she whispered. "Just be careful that word doesn't get out to my other clients."

"Just how many bachelors' houses do you clean?"

Marion smiled at the thought that John could be jealous.

"Not many." Actually, there were only two others and they were both over sixty, but she wasn't about to tell him that. "A girl can't be too cautious, you know."

"Humph." John growled. He led her around the dance floor a few more minutes.

Finally, he said, "Then does that mean you will go out with me?"

"Only if you promise not to tell my other clients."

"That's a promise I can't keep."

Shocked, Marion looked up at him. "Why not?"

John grinned at her. "Because I don't know who they are!"

For all the tulips in Holland, Marion couldn't decide if she was doing the right thing or not. But one thing she did know. She hadn't felt this good in a long time, and even if she were throwing caution to the wind, it was worth it.

John cared about the same things she did. Other than the baseball field, they disagreed about nothing. Frankly, she had to admit—if only to herself—that she had fallen in love with John the first moment they met.

The music stopped.

For the next hour they danced the slow dances, and when they weren't dancing they stood in a corner oblivious to everyone around them. Never before had Marion felt so special. So badly she wanted to believe that John cared for her, more than she dared admit.

At one point, the band took a break. Marion excused herself, stating she was going to the powder room. When she came back, she didn't see John at first. Then she saw him talking with several of his classmates, male and female. With his back to her, he didn't see her approach the group. She heard John's voice.

"Yes, I'm planning to get married in the near future. And I want to have a large family, three boys and three girls."

One of the women said, "With the looks in your family, John, they'll all be beautiful children."

"Naturally," John boasted back.

Marion froze, not hearing the many laughs. Now her skin felt icy; a cold clamminess enveloped her, a coldness unlike anything she'd ever felt before.

If she'd had any doubt that he felt something special for her, those feelings had just been dashed upon a hard and rocky shore. John wouldn't want her once he discovered she couldn't have children. She'd heard him. He expected to have a large family one day. Anything but that she would have granted him. But in this, fate had dealt her an empty hand. There would be no children for her. None that came from her body, that is. And not every man wanted to raise someone else's child.

No matter what happened between her and John, she still intended to adopt. She wanted children that badly. Even if she had to choose between John and a child, she'd pick the child. She could live a life without the love of a man, but she knew she couldn't live without a child.

She lifted her chin, determined not to let this get her down. For a few hours, she had enjoyed the fantasy of her and John dating, even getting married. But it'd been just that—a fantasy.

Though she couldn't produce her own children, there were plenty of children that needed homes, and by this time next year, she expected to have her first child with her.

Tonight was a charade, nothing more than a fantasy that John had wanted to create for his friends. It was easy to understand why he'd wanted to create the illusion, but tonight Marion had learned her own illusion was nothing but air. Illusions looked like magic on the outside, but inside there was just a hollowness that had left her aching. She wanted the magic back.

With a sigh of regret that the magic just wasn't meant for her, she turned to the refreshment table to get a cup of punch and gather her courage to return to John. She had promised to help him out tonight and she didn't want to dampen his party. He'd never know that she had briefly considered their future as a couple.

The band started up and the group John was with dispersed to find their partners. Marion saw John look around, and then he spotted her. His face lit up and he grinned. His eyes beckoned to her as he walked toward her. Despite everything, her heart fluttered.

Her instinct told her to run, but she forced herself to stay in place. Finally John stood in front of her.

Without a word said, John took her hand, raised it to his mouth, then kissed it, his lips barely brushing her sensitive skin. And then he led her to the dance floor.

Unable to say a word, all Marion could do was follow his lead. If the truth were known, she didn't want to be anywhere else but right where she was—in his arms—despite knowing that tomorrow everything would be back to normal again.

She'd been wrong. There was still a little magic left tonight. Mere crumbs. But she was willing to enjoy those crumbs for however long they lasted. And she was willing to risk her heart, knowing there'd be nothing but heartbreak when it was over.

"Thank you," he said.

"For what?"

"For making this a memorable evening. It wouldn't have been the same without you."

All Marion could do was stare at a button on his shirt. "You're welcome," she replied.

John placed a finger under her chin and tilted her head up until she was forced to look at him. He frowned at her. "What's wrong?"

Quickly, she said, "Nothing."

"Something must be wrong. You're not the same."

Marion shrugged, looking at his Adam's apple, unable to continue looking him in the eye. "Just tired, I guess."

"Ready to go?"

Though she really didn't want to go, she knew it'd be for the best. She nodded.

As they walked to the car, her hand engulfed in his, she felt her heart disintegrate into a hundred little pieces. She thought she could do this. She loved him, but she wasn't about to subject him, or anyone else for that matter, to her physical inability. She wouldn't want his dreams shattered any more than hers had already been.

As much as she felt they'd grown closer during this past weekend, their relationship wouldn't go any further than friendship.

Initially, Marion had enjoyed John's reunion. Now, she was glad they were leaving. Her face felt stiff from having to smile, and she had felt so artificial making sure she laughed at the right times and appeared to be enjoying herself so John wouldn't think anything was wrong. In a few more minutes, she could escape to her room at his parents' house. And then, tomorrow, they'd be returning home.

Marion closed her eyes in frustration, realizing the long drive they still had in front of them tomorrow. How would she survive, continuing the pretense?

No, there wouldn't be any pretense. They were friends. That hadn't changed at all.

The rest of the way to his parents' house, Marion didn't have to worry about her noticeable silence. John was exhilarated enough for the both of them, talking of this friend and that, amazed at how well some were doing, appalled at the bad luck of others.

None too soon, and yet at the same time all too soon for Marion, they were pulling in the driveway.

Once they reached the front door, John stopped talking. Marion stood aside while he fitted the key into the door. When the door swung open, she entered first, heading immediately up the stairs to her room. John followed close behind her.

Just as she grabbed hold of the doorknob to her door, John put a hand on her elbow, turning her around.

Nervously, she gazed up at him, just in time to see he was going to kiss her. His lips lightly grazed hers, then he softly said, "Good night, Marion. Sweet dreams."

" 'Night, John," she said, barely at a whisper. Unable to swallow because of the lump in her throat, Marion quickly entered her room, then shut the door leaning against it. She wiped at the wetness on her cheeks. Life just wasn't fair. Just when she thought she was getting her life back on track, her heart derailed her like this.

In the darkness, she walked across the room until she stood in front of the window. Brushing aside the sheer curtain with one hand, she gazed up at the near-full moon. *Better to have loved and lost than never to have loved at all.* She remembered the time her mother said those words to her after Marion had come home from school having broken up with a boyfriend.

Marion sighed. Her mother had been right.

Though she wished things could be different between her and John, she wasn't going to dwell on what couldn't be. Instead, she'd focus on what was.

As she dressed for bed, Marion thought about the evening and the class reunion. Even though John wasn't rich or famous like some of his classmates who were doctors, lawyers, a congressman, a New York ballerina, and a news correspondent who had covered the Persian Gulf War, he was a man who knew what he wanted and enjoyed doing it. And though they had differences regarding the final outcome of the property next to her father's house, Marion admired his determination to help their community's youth. Not many people would do that unless their own children were directly involved.

She remembered at one point in the evening when someone had criticized today's youth. John shot back that not all kids were bad, they just needed an outlet and proper guidance. When someone else had said they weren't his kids, why bother, John had retorted with, "They don't have to be yours for you to care about them. We should care about all the children."

Never had Marion been more proud of anybody than she had been of John at that moment. His desire to help others, particularly the children, was admirable.

But why couldn't he have picked another vacant lot to build his ball field? she thought. She hated that she was part of the problem, rather than part of a solution.

Marion and John left for south Georgia early the next morning. Neither spoke much and Marion was glad. Instead, the radio filled the car with country music. When they had passed through Macon, John said, "Before the season is over, I want to come up to a Braves' game. Maybe you'd like to come too. Oh, I forgot you don't like baseball."

"I never said I didn't like baseball. You're assuming I don't like baseball because I've opposed your plans for the ball field."

"Actually, yes."

"I like baseball."

"But you're just opposed to the placement of the ball field?"

"Yes."

"Even now?"

What did he mean by that? she wondered. As far as she was concerned, nothing had changed. "Yes, even now. I'm not against what you're doing. I'm for keeping the peace and quiet in Dad's neighborhood. There's a difference."

When John didn't pursue the subject further, Marion became puzzled. In the past, he would have tried to persuade her a bit longer, hoping to change her mind. Today, he seemed satisfied with her answer. Glancing at him, she saw him frowning. Any other time, when he talked about the ball field, his whole face would light up. What caused the frown now?

By the time they reached Briar, it was dark. Moments later they were at her father's house. When she reached for her door handle, John's hand on her other arm stopped her.

"Marion, I've done a lot of thinking the past few weeks and this weekend . . . I had fun. I was serious about wanting us to date. I'd like to see more of you."

Before this weekend, those were the words she'd longed to hear. But the weekend had changed everything. "I've given it some more thought, John. I don't think that would be a good idea. Let's just keep things the way they are."

"I can't do that anymore."

"We have to."

"You're saying that because of our differences regarding the ball field."

"We have more differences than you think."

"I don't believe there isn't anything we can't work out."

She didn't want to hurt him, not for anything in this world. "John, I've got too many things going on in my life right now. This isn't a good time for a relationship for me right now," she lied.

If he only knew how much she had longed to hear him say these things. But that was before she'd heard what he had said about wanting a family at the class reunion. She wouldn't be the one to deny him his dreams, even if they had been denied to her.

She knew how disappointing it was to want kids and not be able to have them. How much more difficult would it be for John to be married to her, not able to have their own kids, yet knowing at the same time with anyone else he could have kids.

Artificial insemination wasn't an answer for her. It would kill her to watch someone else grow big with her husband's child. No, adoption was the only way for her.

This time when she reached for the door, John didn't stop her. He got her bag from the backseat, and she bit her tongue when John insisted on escorting her to the front door. Marion was quite aware of the fact, however, that he didn't touch her like he normally did when taking her to the door.

Already their relationship had changed, and it saddened her. There was no going back now. At the door, she turned and reached for her bag. Their hands touched and they froze, staring at each other.

The air was heavy with anticipation. Finally, after what seemed like an eternity to Marion, she tugged on the handle. John released it, immediately shoving his hands into his pants pockets.

"Thanks again. For going with me," he said softly.

Quickly he turned, and was several steps away before she found her voice. "John."

He turned abruptly, his face anxious.

How she wished she could tell him what she herself longed to say. Instead, she said, "Will you be at our last class Wednesday night?"

Realizing she hadn't changed her mind about the dating issue, John thought for a few seconds. "No...no, I don't think so. There's a game that night."

"Oh. Okay." This was it, she thought. "Good night."

John looked at her for another few seconds, then turned and quickly reached the car. Not once did he look back as was his custom. He got into his car and drove off without giving her the opportunity to wave good-bye.

Immediately, Marion wished he'd return.

She'd tell him she'd changed her mind. But his taillights disappeared and the neighborhood was silent.

Determined that she wasn't going to feel sorry for herself, the first thing Marion did upon entering the house and discovering her father hadn't returned, was go to the radio and turn it up, filling the house with music. She sang loudly to the old rock-and-roll lyrics, even though tears ran down her cheeks.

Chapter Nine

The next morning Marion answered the doorbell thinking it was her father and that he'd forgotten his key. Instead, she found Peggy on the porch with an armful of dishes.

"Here, let me help," Marion said, taking several from her. "What's all this?"

"Your dishes. I'm returning them."

"How did you get so many of them? No, don't answer that. I don't think I want to know."

"You know good and well I'm lousy about returning things. If I'd been smart I'd have left them out on the counter for you to pick up, as often as you're at my house. But then

I never do anything the smart way. How was the weekend?"

"Ah, now we come to it. The real reason why you're here."

"Am I that transparent?"

"Like clean glass."

"So how was the weekend? I should hate you for not calling me yesterday, but then I figured you got in late."

Marion nodded and Peggy continued. "But then when you didn't call me today, I knew something was wrong."

"The weekend was fine," Marion said, trying to keep her voice even.

Unfortunately, Marion knew she had shadows under her eyes and knew Peggy had seen them. "I don't believe that for a minute," Peggy said. "Your eyes say you had a lousy time. Give, girl."

"John's family was wonderful. They made me feel like one of the family. And Raleigh is a beautiful community."

"You're beating around the bush. What went wrong? How was the class reunion?"

"Peggy—"

"You want me to go to John and ask him what he did to give you this sad look?"

"Don't you dare!" Marion could feel the

tears welling in her eyes. "He wants us to date."

"But that's good."

Marion shook her head from side to side. "No, it's not. One day he wants to have a large family."

Peggy's bright expression disappeared to be replaced with a more somber expression. "Oh."

"Yeah. Oh."

"When are you going to tell him?" When Marion didn't answer, Peggy probed, "You *are* going to tell him about your accident, aren't you?"

"Peggy, it's much simpler just not to date. He'll be nothing but disappointed if he gets interested in me."

"You're not being fair to yourself or to him. You're not giving him a chance."

"I've got an appointment at the adoption agency next week. That's all the chance I want. This isn't a fairy tale. Life doesn't always have a 'and they lived happily ever after' ending. You ought to know that from what you see in court."

"I also see a lot of people who aren't talking to each other, people who could save a lot of money in attorney fees if they'd only do more talking."

Marion was on the verge of telling her when she suddenly decided she didn't want to share this with Peggy. She had to work this out for herself. Confiding in Peggy wasn't going to change anything. Marion's goals were in place. Now it was just a matter of achieving them. As much as she dearly loved her friend, Peggy's answers weren't always the right ones for her.

Just then her father arrived home. Marion was glad for the interruption, and equally glad when Peggy wasn't able to pursue the subject any further. Her father told of his adventures at Panama Beach and how Betty and he had spent most of their time fishing off the piers.

Shortly after Peggy left, Marion left too, telling her father she needed to deliver some supplies to the Home Economics room for tonight's class.

Marion passed the woodworking shop, surprised to see half a dozen men in there working on what appeared to be benches.

Not thinking too much about it, she continued down to the classroom and set about unloading her groceries. About ten minutes later she heard voices through her open doorway, out in the hallway.

"I for one plan to make use of these

benches we're making. I'm tired of carrying lawn chairs to these games."

"Hard to believe the coach finally got City Hall to agree to the new park."

Marion frowned, at first thinking they were talking about John. Just as quickly, however, she decided they were talking about someone and something else. She would have heard otherwise. Gossip was too rampant in the community for her not to have heard about any changes. But then again, she'd been busy lately.

"John sure is a smooth talker," another voice chortled. "Even I was opposed to that park, especially with all them old folks around. But the more I listened, the more he made sense."

The package of cheese in her hand forgotten, Marion took a few steps closer to the door. A chill washed over her. It couldn't be. It just couldn't be.

Unable to finish the necessary preparations for tonight's class, Marion quickly stored the perishables in the refrigerator and drove home. When she turned off the ignition, she realized she had no memory of driving home. Concerned about the implications of what she'd just heard, she'd driven home by rote.

Entering the house, she quickly saw she was alone. Not able to sit still, she went and made lemonade and poured herself a glass. Now it sat on the table, condensation pooling in a watery puddle around the glass.

The moment she heard the back door open, she shot out of her chair and met her dad at the door.

"Dad? We've got to get down to City Hall before they close. I heard John—"

Gently, he said, "Sit down, Marion."

She frowned seeing her father's serious expression. The last time he looked like this was when he had to tell her that her mother was sick and dying.

He continued, "We should have had this talk a while back. I was hoping to talk to you before you found out."

"You mean it's true? But I thought... John was behind all this, wasn't he?"

"You're wrong, Marion. At first as a group—as a neighborhood—we were against the ballpark. Any time there's change, people balk. But as a neighborhood, we've had several meetings. We changed our minds and this is what we want."

"You want the noise?"

"We want the young people. There's a difference. Look at the neighborhood from our eyes. Sure, it's quiet. It's peaceful. But it's also dead. We want the added activity the ball field will bring. You may not be aware of it, Marion, but many of these folks around here have grandkids, grandkids that live elsewhere. We may be old—"

"Dad, you're not old."

"Yes, I am. But only in body. In spirit I'm just as young as I always was. You'll understand that as you get older. What I'm getting to is that as a neighborhood we want the ballpark. We want the youth."

"What about the trash, the debris, that will be left behind after the games?"

"I don't think it'll be a problem. Not when you consider the park will be surrounded with flower beds and gardens, and lots of decorated trash cans. We see this park as an asset to the neighborhood, not as a detriment. And it's been arranged that we, as a neighborhood, are going to be partners in the concession stand. The women want to supply cookies and other snacks. The money we earn will be placed in a fund for those less fortunate who need it."

"Sounds like it's all been thought out."

"Thanks to John. He only wants what's best for everyone. He really cares about these kids—all kids—and he's right about one thing. We have to care about our young people enough that we're willing to make changes. This is just a small thing for us, and yet it will mean a few more kids off the streets, away from crime and drugs. If a park can give these kids a few hours of pleasure, then we're doing the right thing even with the occasional noise and bright lights. Heck, I've got to say, I'm looking forward to it."

As she listened to her dad's speech, Marion wondered at what point she'd lost sight of the people around her. Tunnel vision of her own pain, her own loss, had blinded her to the feelings of others, including her own father. And worst of all, as she looked back over the whole situation now, she saw that she had appeared anti-child. That thought disturbed her more than anything, for all her life she had loved children. Still did. If she didn't, she wouldn't be going back to teaching this fall.

Because of her accident...no, she couldn't blame anything anymore on the accident. It was in the past. The future was where she was headed and now there was no looking back.

Her father continued, "We didn't give John much of a chance in the beginning. We turned him out without really listening." Marion knew her father was saying the same thing Peggy had earlier—that people needed to talk.

Eventually her father had listened to John, and now, consequently, a change was occurring peacefully. "John came to see some of us individually, then later after we understood his deep commitment, he came to our neighborhood meetings as a concerned individual. We never invited you to those meetings, sweetheart, because you're not one of the homeowners. I understand your concern and greatly appreciate that you were acting on my behalf, but you were wrong. And you're wrong to let this difference between you and John keep you apart."

"Dad, our differences—"

"Are overruling your heart. I'm no more blind to the feelings you two share, than you were to my feelings for Betty. It's hard to keep wearing a mask all the time. It's not my intention to pry, and I won't ask. You know I'm always ready to listen, though, anytime you want to talk."

Marion got up and kissed his cheek. "I know, Dad. And I appreciate it."

"There's something else I want to talk to

you about. Betty and I want to get married, and we want your approval."

"Oh, Dad, you don't need my approval."

"That's what I told Betty, but she wants you included in the decision. That's just the way she is and one of the reasons why I love her."

"How about a celebration dinner this weekend? My treat."

"Only if it's your famous fried chicken and you show Betty your secret."

Marion laughed. "It's a deal."

"There's something else," he added. "Betty and I decided I'm going to live with her. We want you to stay here."

"But don't you want to sell the house?"

"Only if you don't want it. I'd prefer to give it to you."

"Dad, I'm honored, and I'd love to have the house, but I can't afford it. Not with the new business and all."

"Honey, I don't think you understand. It's my gift to you. Provided, of course, I always have a place to come whenever I'm in the doghouse with Betty."

Marion laughed. "*You* in the doghouse?"

"There's always a first time."

* * *

Two hours later Marion returned to the high school. She was early tonight as she needed to finish what she'd neglected to do earlier. Tonight her students were in for a special treat—a strawberry soufflé. But first, she needed to do some advance preparation.

John was the first to arrive. The moment she saw him in the doorway, her pulse fluttered.

"Hi," she said, determined to keep their conversation away from her personal feelings. "Ready to graduate tonight?"

"Hardly," John responded. When he stood across the counter from her, it was all she could do to keep her hands from shaking.

"Though I can now cook a few meals without scorching them." He looked at her with a longing that told her if given the opportunity, he'd ask the questions she didn't want to answer.

Granted, he deserved some answers, but Marion didn't want that conversation to take place until after the class was over. She wanted her full attention directed for the next couple of hours to making the best soufflé possible.

It was going to be a miracle, however, if she could pull it off. Just smelling John's spicy after-shave was playing havoc on her ability to concentrate. What would it be like during class, knowing he was standing so close, so close she could smell his cologne?

"You'll get better," she told him. She gave the batter she was beating with a wooden spoon her total attention while she talked. "And you'll feel more and more confident as you cook." If only she could feel confident about tonight—during class and later.

"Marion, is something wrong?"

Startled, Marion glanced at him, then forced her gaze back down to the bowl. "Wrong? There's nothing wrong." With a false brightness she didn't feel, she said. "I'm fine."

Just then, much to Marion's relief, several other students arrived and started talking with John, forcing him to leave Marion's side. She knew she couldn't postpone the inevitable—she'd have to talk with John tonight. Telling him the truth would be the hardest thing she ever had to do. It would hurt him, but it'd be better for him to find out now than several months down the road.

Later, after all the students had each come up to her at the end of the class, telling her how much they had enjoyed the class and hoped she'd teach another, it was now just she and John left in the room.

He still sat at his table, his empty paper plate in front of him, eyeballing her as if waiting for her to escape.

Instead, she took off her apron, laid it on the counter, then went and sat opposite him.

For a few seconds neither of them said anything. Marion stared at her clasped hands wondering how to begin, and John fidgeted with his fork.

"I heard you—"

"John, there's something—"

They both spoke at the same time.

Wanting to postpone her news until the last possible moment, Marion said, "Go ahead."

"I heard you've got a teaching position."

"As an English teacher at the high school. When you told me about the football players who might not be able to play because of their grades, it got me thinking."

"I had no idea you were a teacher."

"I know. I meant to tell you."

"Why didn't you?"

"Too much else was happening, which is what I want to talk to you about now. I want to apologize about the ballpark. I understand everything's been settled. I'm glad everything's worked out. I was wrong. It wasn't my place to fight you on it like I did. I know that now. Dad's excited about it—I imagine you are too."

"For the kids I am. It's going to be a lot of hard work getting it ready, but all in all I'll enjoy it." He studied her for a moment. When he moved his hands toward hers, Marion pulled back. He sat back in his chair, puzzled. "Something happened at the class reunion, didn't it? Ever since that night you've been different."

"There's something I need to tell you. Something I should have told you that night."

"I'm listening."

"Before I came here I was teaching in Atlanta. My life was perfect. I enjoyed my job, the kids I taught. I loved my apartment. And I was engaged to get married."

She studied John to watch his reaction. Other than his eyebrows knitting together, he had none. His gaze was steady and probing. She shook off the feeling that he could see her very soul.

"A little over a year ago, I was in a accident. It left me sterile, unable to have children. When my fiancé found out, he left me."

Marion paused, expecting him to express

the words most other people did. When he didn't say anything at all, Marion continued. "I came home to heal, with every intention of going back to Atlanta." She stared off at the distance, remembering. "But my recovery took longer than I thought it would, and the more time that passed, the less I wanted to go back. In the meantime, I started Maid Marion."

Looking at John again, she said, "That more or less brings me up to now."

"Whatever happened to your fiancé?"

Marion shrugged. "I don't know."

"Do you care?"

"Not really. Not anymore. At first I was terribly hurt, but now I realize he wasn't the right man for me. Of course, I didn't truly accept everything—the accident nor our breakup—until recently. I wanted to ignore it all—blame someone when there was no one to blame. Plus I felt sorry for myself for far too long."

"What changed your mind? I mean, what was the turning point?"

"When I met Billy. I realized just because I couldn't have children, that didn't mean there weren't other options that would allow me to have children. I'm teaching again so I can adopt a child of my own. I need a job that's a bit more stable than my newly formed business."

"That still doesn't explain what happened the night of the class reunion."

Marion wasn't sure how to progress at this moment. Did she lay everything out in the open, taking the chance that she could have been wrong about his feelings, thus exposing herself to . . . whatever? Or did she hide her true feelings, thus never learning the truth about how John felt?

Never one to gamble in the past, Marion decided to take a chance this time. She had absolutely nothing to lose at this point. As far as she was concerned, John was never hers to start with. How could she lose him if she never had him? Her ego and her pride might take a bruising, but far better to have a few bruises than to later discover she had thrown everything away.

"I enjoyed the weekend, John. We had something special." As much as she wanted to suggest that she thought he'd been on the verge of proposing, she couldn't bring herself to say it out loud. What if she was wrong? What if she made a complete fool of herself? Not once had he said he loved her.

Other than the tight line his mouth had

become, she couldn't tell a thing from his expression. If only he would say something. Reassure her.

No, she thought. That would be wrong. It wasn't his job to reassure her. She had to depend on herself. In order to raise a child as a single parent, she had to be strong. She would have to be both mother and father to this child. A daunting task, but she was capable, and she'd succeed.

"We did have something special." He looked a bit sad. "And then something happened, but I never knew what it was."

The time was now. Marion took a deep breath and plunged ahead. "I overheard you tell some others that you wanted a large family. I couldn't let you fall in love with me knowing I couldn't have children. And I didn't want to have to hurt you by turning you down. I'm sorry, John. As much as I love you, it wouldn't work."

He stood, walked the distance of the room, his footsteps hard and brittle in the otherwise quiet building. With his hands jammed in his pockets, he spun around. "Just like that?" He glared at her. "You decided! You didn't even give me a chance. If you loved me as much as you say you did, wouldn't you have at least given my feelings consideration? Didn't I have the right to make a decision about my future—our future—by knowing all the facts?"

Stunned at his anger, Marion blinked. "I ...I was considering your feelings. I knew how you felt about wanting children of your own. I'm not the person for you."

"You presume too much. First the ball field, now this. You don't live in a nice safe bubble, but yet you're sure as heck trying to insulate yourself from feeling any pain."

Marion gasped.

John ran a hand through his hair in frustration.

"Marion, I'm sorry. That came out wrong. I didn't mean to imply that you weren't entitled to pain—not with all you've been through." He paused, studying her, debating whether to say anything more. He added, "But you can't plan your future without involving others around you. You don't live in a vacuum. A happy person is a connected person. It's like a telephone line. Without connections you're just talking into an empty phone. No one's on the other end."

Again, he ran his hand through his hair. Marion was stunned. She couldn't say a word. She couldn't believe John was saying these things to her.

"I've said more than I should. I love you, Marion. But I want to marry someone who can be honest with me. I wish you nothing but the best. I hope you find what it is you're looking for."

Quickly, he left the room. The sound of the big double outer doors shutting behind him echoed in the hallway.

Dismayed at the turn of events, Marion lay her head down, her forehead resting on her arms, wanting to do nothing but cry.

But she couldn't. She was too stunned at the turn of events. She had been wrong, so wrong.

She sighed heavily. Much of what John had said was true. She had presumed too much. She wasn't clairvoyant, a mind reader, and yet she'd made a decision based on what *she* thought John wanted.

Peggy had said it. Her father had said it. And even now John had said it: Unless people were willing to talk and come to an understanding, nothing got resolved.

She hadn't talked with her dad about the park, but just assumed he didn't want it any more than she did. Not once, throughout the ordeal, did she discuss it further with him. Had she done so, she would have found out a lot earlier on about her father's change of heart. Of how the entire neighborhood had rallied around John.

Her bridges were certainly burned now. Without knowing it, John had been hers, but she'd blown it. He had loved her. And now he was gone.

Not that she blamed him. If someone had presumed to do her thinking for her, she'd have been just as angry.

Dazed, Marion finished locking up. It took her twice as long as normal because her muscles wouldn't cooperate, plus her mind kept straying. She felt as if someone had drugged her.

When she got home, she was glad to see that her father was gone. She didn't want to explain to him how she'd mishandled the whole relationship with John. Though she knew her father would have been understanding and gentle, she just couldn't face him right now. Tonight, she couldn't face anyone.

Storing the perishables in the refrigerator and leaving everything else on the counter, Marion went upstairs, her movements wooden and slow. All she wanted to do was reach the safe haven of her room.

Once there, she sprawled across her bed, face down, and finally cried.

Chapter Ten

Saturday, Marion woke dreading getting out of bed. Today was the last time she'd be cleaning John's apartment. All week long, she had found herself looking for him on the street or in the stores, but at the same time, hoping she wouldn't run in to him.

During the past week, she'd driven past North Elementary School at times she thought he'd be practicing, but at no time was there anyone on the playgrounds. Not that she could see it from the road. Nor was she about to stop and get out of the car. Each time she found herself straining to see if he or any of his players were back there, she chastised herself for even looking.

She'd blown it—the relationship was over and done with. She had to get over him.

The only way to get past today, and the awkwardness of cleaning his apartment, was to get up and get it done.

Kicking back the sheets, Marion jumped out of bed and threw on her clothes. It wouldn't do her any good lying in bed procrastinating or even thinking about what she had to do. All she had to do was do it.

His car wasn't in the usual spot, she noted as she parked her car. When she knocked on his door there was no answer.

Hesitantly, she opened the door, peeking around the corner, not sure what to expect. Nothing but silence greeted her.

Grateful that he was gone, Marion scurried into the apartment and shut the door, bolting it securely. As if that would keep him out, she thought. He did have a key after all.

Marion was surprised to see the apartment relatively clean. There was hardly anything for her to do. The towels were all washed, folded, and put away. Clean sheets were on the bed. And the kitchen was nearly spotless. He even had a casserole in the refrigerator that was obviously tonight's dinner. She felt as useless as a sponge in a flood.

In less than an hour, she was done. Taking the original contract out of her bag, she signed it, stating the contractual agreement was complete, and left a copy on his desk. On top of it, she left his key.

At the door, she took one last lingering look around. Wishing things had turned out differently, but knowing there was no going back, Marion shut the door quietly behind her.

With her hand still on the doorknob, she looked at the door recognizing the symbolism it held for her. She had just closed the door on another chapter of her life, and she was about to begin another.

The next two weeks were busy ones for Marion. She spent all her time training the two women who were now working part-time for her. One was a mother who wanted to work only while her children were in school. The other woman was elderly, wanting something to do but didn't want to wear herself out doing it.

Quickly, the two women caught on, and Marion felt secure that the actual work was in good hands. All that remained for her to do was the bookkeeping and maintenance of the customer files. Because of her two employees, she found there was more bookkeeping to do, but nothing that couldn't be handled in a few hours a week.

Evenings were the worst for her. Once the dinner dishes were done, there wasn't much to do except read and watch old movies. The movies were all romances and made her feel worse than she already did.

Several evenings she had spent with her father and Betty, helping them plan their wedding—at their insistence—but her heart wasn't in it. She promised to do the catering and helped plan the menu, but beyond that there wasn't much else for her to do.

Most of the time, she spent her evenings—after the sun had set—out on the porch, in the swing, leisurely moving back and forth. Her view was of the neighborhood and what would eventually be the ball field. Little by little improvements were being made to the lot. It'd been mowed and baselines put in. Benches and a fence behind home plate had been installed. At night, after the heat of the day, some of the area residents could be seen working on the grounds where the flower beds would eventually go. Though there was a lot of work yet to be done, the improvements were good. Actually, Marion had to admit, it appeared as if the ball field had been there forever.

Though she knew it wasn't doing her mind, nor her heart, any good, all she could do was stare at the field. It was a reminder of everything she'd done wrong. But she didn't wallow in pity or become maudlin about it. She forgave herself for making the mistake, vowing she would never again presume to know what another person wanted without asking them first.

Finally one night, determined to do something, Marion went in and planned a year's worth of cooking courses she could teach at home. Holiday cookies. St. Valentine's Day candies. Cake decorating. Putting together the perfect picnics. As she looked at the classes she'd planned, it dawned on her that nearly every class dealt with either sweets for a loved one or celebrating with a family.

She threw her pencil down and pushed her chair back. It was going to take her a long time to get over John.

The following day, she returned to Thomasville and the adoption agency. Earlier in the week, Marion had called Stephanie

Morris, explaining her life-style changes. Stephanie had told her it was time to come in and fill out an application.

An hour later, Marion stood on the street, mentally hugging herself. She was going to have a child. Right now she didn't know if it'd be a girl or a boy or what age he or she would be, but to Marion, it didn't matter. Any child would be welcomed and thoroughly loved.

Marion thought about calling Peggy, but remembered Peggy was out of town. Her husband had surprised Peggy with an anniversary gift to Paris. They were due back home in two weeks.

The following week, Marion returned to school along with the rest of the teachers, readying her class, anxious for the following Monday to arrive. She didn't know who was going to be more nervous, she or her students.

Now it was Saturday again. Marion was on the porch enjoying the early morning breeze. Though it was September, the day was forecast to be muggy and hot. She was tired from the changes that had occurred in the last few weeks, but it was a delicious kind of tired.

She pushed off with her foot, the swing

creaking as it moved back and forth. The only other sounds were those of the birds chirping in the trees. Then she heard the motor of a car.

Figuring it was a neighbor, she didn't bother to twist her head to see who it was. The car passed her peripheral vision, then parked at the boundary line between her father's house—her house now, since he'd deeded it over to her—and the empty lot next door.

Her foot froze, the swing wobbled drunkenly, and her heart accelerated at the sight of John getting out of the car. Not once in all these weeks had she seen him.

He looked good, and her gaze didn't waver as she stared at him. Finally, he looked her way. They stared at each other. Her heartbeat kicked into high gear.

Not knowing if she should go into the house or not, Marion decided she'd be a coward if she were to go in.

Finally, John moved, opening his trunk. He pulled out a martin house and a telescopic pole. He started walking toward her.

Panic welled in her throat. She swallowed heavily. What would she say?

Finally, there was nowhere to go. He

turned and came up to the porch. "Hello," he said.

"Hello," she replied huskily. He looked thinner, but just as good as he ever did.

"I finally finished your dad's martin house."

"He'll love it. Thank you."

John set it down on the porch, leaning the pole against the rail. "Is it okay if I sit down?"

Nervous as a cat about to forge a raging river, she nodded.

He sat in a chair that faced her. "How have you been?" he asked.

"Fine," she answered. "Some days good, some worse."

This time it was John's turn to nod.

Marion hated the awkwardness of their conversation. She didn't like their being apart like this. There were going to be other times when he'd be next door with his boys playing ball. If nothing else, she wanted them to be friends again.

It was time to put everything on the line. She had to tell him the truth. If nothing else, she had learned that from her past mistakes. "I've missed you."

"I've missed you too. That's why I'm here."

Hope grew in her heart.

"I want to negotiate another contract with you."

Despair plunged her heart to the basement of her soul. "Sure," she said evenly, disguising the hurt she felt because he wanted the services of Maid Marion.

Instantly, she regretted her despair. They were talking again. Just moments ago, she'd told herself if nothing else, she wanted them to be friends. Now they were friends again. She rose from the swing. "Let me go into the house and get a contract. Though I've got to warn you, I won't be the one doing the actual cleaning. I've hired two women who do the work, because I'm teaching now."

She had barely taken a step when he grabbed her hand. "I know. But I don't want them. I want you."

The swing bumped into the back of her leg. She frowned at him. "I just told you, I can't—"

With the speed of lightning, he moved over to the swing, pulling her down next to him. "That contract you've got inside won't work for what I want."

She was acutely aware that his fingers were rubbing the bare skin on her arm. The breath caught in her lungs. Their eyes locked. He studied her, silently daring her to ask the question.

Finally, she did. "What is it that you want?"

"For you to be my wife."

Marion gasped. "But—"

"I know. You can't have any children. Don't you know that all the children in the world—even if they were my very own flesh and blood—wouldn't mean anything to me if you weren't there too? I love you. And I'll love any children we adopt. I'll love you even if we never adopt. I want to spend the rest of my life with you. What do you say?"

"Show me where to sign on the dotted line."

John hugged her and gave her a resounding kiss, putting his seal on the contract.

A few seconds later, Marion said, "Wait until we tell Dad. He's getting married in two weeks."

"Maybe we can make it a double wedding," John said. "I don't want to wait any longer than that myself."

"Neither do I," Marion said. "Neither do I."